TOO MANY BULLETS!

Slade's thoughts were abrubtly broken off by an outburst of firing from the rockpile. One flurry of shots, seconds later another. Splintered and powdered stone flew up in his face as slugs whistled off in scattered directions.

Slade squirmed hurriedly backward, raised himself on knees and elbows and started to scrabble to his right.

The movement saved his life.

The slug that tore through the fleshy part of his left upper arm seared across his chest instead of blasting through his ribs to his heart . . .

Turning, squirming forward, dragging his numb left arm, Slade looked toward the rockpile. *Three riders were coming hell-bent toward him . . . .*

HORSETHIEF CANYON

Jerry Brucker

LEISURE BOOKS   NEW YORK CITY

Chapter 1

Slade Shelbourne stared down on desolation.

Arid, sun-baked, sandy earth. Thin scattering of mostly leafless brush. Sparse clusters of prickly-pear cactus, gray and withered.

And rocks. Rocks of all sizes and shapes.

Slade's elbows, knees and hip bones ached from long contact with the unyielding surface of one of the rocks. A big, flat-topped specimen, one of thousands of gray-tan boulders that formed an escarpment along the north rim of the arroyo.

His mind backtracked half a dozen years, recalled a youth of 18 whose comfortably padded body would have provided better protection against the hard rock. But that was a war and a military prison ago, and more than half a continent away. Now there wasn't an ounce of excess flesh in the 160 pounds of bone, muscle, viscera, cartilage and skin that made up his six-foot-two frame.

If there had been any spare flesh it would have melted away during three and a half days following a trail through the near-waterless wilderness of the Baja California frontier. What little moisture remained in his body was now being rapidly dehydrated by the mid-August noon sun blazing down from a cloudless blue-white sky.

Cracked lips and spitless mouth made him think of the water in his two canteens, filled that morning from scum-covered pools hollowed into a slab of rock in the bed of a dry wash that, during rare winter rains, briefly became a stream. And from the water's stench Slade suspected either the men or animals had replaced some of the liquid they took.

But recycled or not, the water was wet, and he'd drunk worse at Fort Delaware. Slade decided it was time for a drink, both for his own sake and Lady's.

First, however, he squirmed forward a little to get a better look into the arroyo.

Gazing down, he was struck by the contrast between this barren wasteland and the lush fields, graceful trees and meandering streams of his homeland, the Bluegrass region of Kentucky.

Yet even in this desolation there was an oasis of sorts. A strip of cultivated land about a hundred yards wide by fifty deep. On the left was a bedraggled beanfield; on the right a straggly cornfield; in the middle a small adobe house with lean-to kitchen tacked on behind. Beyond the house, on the bank of the wide dry river bed, was a rickety windmill. On the beanfield side of the house cactus growing close together formed three sides of a small corral, the house making the fourth.

In the corral were five horses and a mule.

Four of the horses were stocky California ponies. The fifth was a rangy blood bay with fine Thoroughbred head and long, slim Thoroughbred legs.

Slade looked at those legs anxiously. As near as

he could tell, they were sound. Anger flared in him. If he'd brought Warrior Prince all the way from Jessamine County, only to have some Mexican horsethieves lame him out here in this rock-jumbled Baja wilderness—

But, though dust dimmed the sheen of his rich red coat, the colt appeared all right. Not even tired from covering almost a hundred and fifty miles with scant feed and water. He held his head high, looking out over the cactus.

The horse was looking, Slade realized, straight up at him on the arroyo rim, scarcely a hundred feet above and a hundred yards away. The breeze was quartering in from the northwest—was Prince getting his scent—or Lady's?

Slade started to scramble backwards, but stopped as a man stepped through the open doorway of the house.

A skinny dog scurried out of the way, scrawny chickens scattered as the man—the first sign of human life Slade had seen in almost three hours of watching—walked out from under the pole-supported thatch ramada that shaded the front of the house. When he stepped into the light, Slade sucked in his breath.

He'd expected a small, dark man—like most of the Baja Californios, a Mexican of predominantly Indian blood.

But this man was big—taller even than Slade—and much heavier. His face and hands, though sun and wind-tanned, were too light for a Mexican, and an unkempt straggle of pale blond hair hung below a flat-crowned gray hat, almost to the collar of his blue-gray shirt.

Again, as in the plaza of San Diego a week before, Slade felt a twinge of recognition. Again, he wished he could get a better look at the big man. Then it had been only a fleeting glimpse in the crowd. Now the distance was too great.

It can't be, he told himself now—as he had then—though with less certainty. He squirmed closer to the edge of the rock.

But down below the man turned away, looked toward the corral. Following his gaze, Slade saw Prince again raise that handsome head with the white diamond squarely between the eyes, look up toward the arroyo rim—and this time the colt peeled back his lips and let out a shrill whinny.

The big man swung around, looked up, but Slade caught only a split-second flash of his face as he shoved himself back, leaped down off the rock, grabbed Lady's upflung head and clamped his fingers over her nostrils to stifle an answering neigh.

"No, girl—hush now," he whispered. "Sure, that's Prince down there—but we don't want him to know we're up here. Not just yet."

When he was satisfied that the mare would be quiet, Slade released her head. Reaching up on the rock, he grabbed the broad-brimmed, high-crowned hat he'd bought in San Antone. The high crown was good for keeping the head cool in desert heat and watering horses, but no good at all for sneaking looks at horsethieves over the edge of flat rocks.

He made horse-watering use' of the hat now,

scooping a canteen out from the shade of an overhanging rock, taking a few swallows for himself, then emptying the remainder into the upturned hat. He held the hat while Lady dipped her muzzle into the water and slurped it up.

When she finished, he tightened the cinch he had loosened earlier—bad enough to leave a horse standing under saddle in this heat. But now, if the man at the ranch had caught a glimpse of him—

"Might have to light out in a hurry, girl," he muttered, patting the mare's well-muscled shoulder.

Like Prince, Lady was a bay, but much darker—more liver than blood. Color wasn't the only difference. Though slightly smaller, Lady—full name Shelbourne Lady—was more solidly built than Prince. Almost blocky, with broad chest, heavy-muscled shoulders and hindquarters. But the fine head with its narrow blaze, the slender, ground-devouring legs, proclaimed her just as much a Thoroughbred. In fact they were close kin, Lady's dam, Gallant Lady, being a daughter of Prince's sire, Warrior King.

Anger rose again in Slade as he thought of Warrior King. Which was worse, Mexican horsethieves or Union Army horsethieves?

Well, he'd given up the great stallion as gone for good. If he hadn't been killed at one of the late-war battlefields—Spotsylvania Court House, Yellow Tavern, Cedar Creek—he was in some ex-Union officer's barn.

But his son, Warrior Prince, Slade could get back. Damn well would get back, if it meant going down to that miserable excuse for a rancho and smoking down all four of those Mexican horse-thieves.

Correction. At least one of the horsethieves wasn't Mexican. That much seemed certain, whether or not the big yellow-haired man was Linc Weaver.

Linc Weaver. The name conjured up mixed memories. His one-time friend, later betrayer and finally—at Fort Delaware—his jailer-tormentor.

Slade pulled his Ball carbine from its upright cavalry-style boot and climbed back up on the flat rock. Removing his hat again, holding the carbine flat in front of him, he inched forward to look over the edge.

The man was gone. The dog was a sand-colored patch on the shade-darkened dust under the ramada. In the corral, Prince was gingerly testing the cactus enclosure, nudging the flat leaves lightly with his nose, jerking back as the barbs pricked him. The colt was unfamiliar with the spiny growth. They'd passed through plenty of desert during the latter stages of that ten-week trek from Kentucky, but Slade had always picketed his two Thoroughbreds clear of cactus.

An ironic grin flickered briefly over his slender but firm-jawed face. All the trouble he'd gone to, all the precautions he'd taken.

One man traveling alone with two such horses was an inviting target for the scum that swarmed through the post-war West. Not to mention the bands of still unconfined Indians who coveted horses as much for food as for transportation.

But a man alone could travel faster than a wagon train. So, after leaving Little Rock Slade had avoided settlements, except when he needed supplies or information about the route ahead. He had taken a south Texas route not so much traveled by emigrants, therefore not so diligently patrolled by always thieving, often murdering Indians. He used tactics learned on Confederate cavalry raids—keeping a watchful eye on his backtrail, picking well-hidden campsites, building only small cooking fires, sleeping with one hand on the carbine.

All this, and then to have Prince stolen right out of the barn at Don Ricardo Castillo's Rancho Los Robles.

Slade remembered the feeling of sick surprise that wrenched his insides when, in the pre-sunrise gloom of the dankly cool 'dobe barn, he looked into Prince's makeshift stall and found it empty. And then, after a short search, found the Indian stable boy, Jesus, behind a pile of sacked grain, gagged and bound with a braided rawhide reata.

"Cuatro hombres, senor," the boy said when Slade removed the gag. "Con pistoles y rifles—"

In almost two months of travel through country long ruled by Spain, and more than a week in San Diego, Slade had picked up a smattering of Spanish—enough to understand that four men with pistols and rifles had stolen Prince.

Inwardly he cursed all the talk, even the newspaper article in Mr. Gatewood's San Diego Union, about the coming match race between Warrior Prince and Don Jose Sandoval's horse Diablo Negro, proclaimed by its owner the champion of both Californias. The race that would, if Prince won, accomplish the purpose of Slade's trip—to win enough money racing his Thoroughbreds against the Arabian-Spanish bloodstock of which the Californios were so proud to pay off the mortgage on Shelbourne Farm back in Kentucky.

When details of the race were announced—including the date, September 15, a Sunday—the residents of San Diego had split into two camps, American and Californio. Argument as to the respective merits of the two contenders flared in the plaza, in stores and shops, in restaurants—such as they were—and bars of the leading hotels—Franklin House, Congress, American, Seeley's new Cosmopolitan. Those arguing frequently backed their beliefs with cash, at constantly fluctuating odds.

To get away from the excitement, Slade had accepted Don Ricardo's invitation to train Prince for the race at his isolated rancho straddling the border a long day's ride from town.

When Prince disappeared, Slade discovered another advantage of the rancho's isolation. If the colt had been stolen in San Diego, he wouldn't have known which direction to search. Here, young Jesus soon found the fresh tracks of five horses—four unshod, one shod—headed south.

Slade had known at a glance the shod horse was Prince. As a yearling, galloping in one of Shelbourne Farm's spacious paddocks, the colt had stepped on a stone, breaking off a piece of his near hind hoof. The hoof had grown back unevenly, so it was necessary to crimp the outer end of the shoe to fit. The print of that crimped shoe was plain in the morning-mist-dampened dirt.

Minutes later Slade had been following the trail mounted on Lady, a sack of grain under his blanket roll behind the cantle, two canteens hanging from the pommel, biscuits, shredded dried beef and coffee in the saddlebags, with two boxes of shells each for the carbine and his Colt's Navy revolver. Fifty caliber for the carbine, thirty-six for the Colts. A Bowie knife in the sheath on his left hip.

Following the trail *alone*. Don Ricardo and his son, Miguel, after escorting Jeff to Los Robles two days before, had headed back to San Diego the next morning. Manuel, the Los Robles mayordomo, and the rancho's four Indian vaqueros had ridden out that same afternoon to drive cattle up into higher country to the north and east. That left at the rancho only Jesus and the cook—his mother.

The horsethieves' tracks—*why*, Slade had wondered, *did it take four men to steal one horse?* —skirted the clustered stick-and-brush huts of an Indian village, crossed a dry river bed and followed a little-used trail southwest into barren, rock-strewn hills. It climbed to a tortuously twisting route up a canyon, topped out on a barren summit. After miles of winding along hump-backed ridges and sparsely vegetated mesas it descended to a broad, treeless valley.

The midmorning sun hot on his shoulders, Slade had pulled up and scanned the valley.

How close was he to his quarry?

Jesus, asleep in the barn, had no idea what time it had been when a rifle barrel jabbed him in the stomach. But he said he lay bound and gagged "muchas horas"—many hours—before Slade found him. The moon had been nearly full, the night clear. The horsethieves could have several hours start. Unless they'd stopped along the way.

They *had*, Slade found as he started to cross the valley. In a dry wash they had dug down for water. Sand in the hole was still damp. Horse droppings and butts of dark brown cigarillos indicated they had spent some time. There were even the still-warm ashes of a small fire—for heating morning coffee?

Slade had scooped out coarse sand until enough water seeped into the hole to form a shallow pool and had let Lady drink. He had fastened his reata around her neck, removed the bridle, and driven a steel picket stake into the ground so she could browse on the meager brush and dried-out grass. When they'd first hit the desert his Thoroughbreds showed little liking for the various forms of chaparral. But they had learned through necessity.

Slade had munched on a biscuit and some of the tough, stringy meat, drunk from a canteen and re-placed the water from the hole. Made himself a cigarette and sprawled in the partial shade of a sparse bush. When the butt singed his fingers he flipped it away, put the bridle back on Lady, swung into the saddle and started across the valley.

Following the trail toward the rugged hills ahead, Slade had felt uneasy. The horsethieves were making no effort to hide their tracks. Were they luring him into ambush?

When the trail started up a winding canyon he had gone cautiously, occasionally reining Lady up to listen for sounds ahead—hearing none. Several times, as the canyon became steeper and narrower, he had dismounted, tied Lady to a bush—he hadn't yet been able to train either Thoroughbred to stand groundreined as western horses did—and scouted ahead. But each time the precaution proved unnecessary.

When the trail finally topped out on a high desert mesa Slade, squinting into mid-afternoon glare, could see nothing of the horsethieves. Nor did he for the rest of that day, or, after spending the night in dry camp behind a big rock, the next day, though hoofprints—including Prince's crimped hind shoe—indicated they were still ahead.

About noon of the second day the trail dropped into another valley and he had found another water hole scooped out in a sandy stream bed. Slade watered Lady, filled the canteens and sat in the shade of a scrub oak for a couple of hours while the mare browsed.

Then he had ridden down the long valley, up through another canyon to a summit. Suddenly there was a salty dampness in the breeze and the chaparral became thicker—through a gunsight gap in broken hills he glimpsed shiny blue. Another hour and he could see a broad expanse of ocean and, far out, two islands.

The sun was nearing the horizon when the trail had intersected what Slade knew must be El

Camino Real, where the broadening canyon melded into seaside plain.

It hadn't looked like much, this King's Highway that since the coming of Captain Portola and Padre Serra almost a hundred years before had been the only land link between Alta California and Mexico. The road that covered more than a thousand miles from San Francisco in the north to Loreto on the Sea of Cortez in the south was scarcely a cart-track wide here. The surface was mostly powdery dust bearing a tracery of hoofmarks.

But plain in the dust again had been that crimped shoe—still headed South.

Slade had pushed on until after dark, making another dry camp at the north end of a big bay guarded on the south by a massive stepped-pyramid headland.

Up and riding early the next day, he had arrived by midmorning at a substantial rancho near the base of the headland.

A thin, scar-faced man carrying an ancient but still functional flintlock had stepped from the doorway of a long, low 'dobe house. The rifle's barrel had been almost in line with Slade's head.

Dropping his hand to the butt of the Colt, Slade had reminded himself that twenty years earlier the United States and Mexico had been at war.

"Buenos dias, amigo," he had said softly.

The scarfaced man had scowled. "Que quiere aqui, hombre?" (What did he want here?)

"Agua—para mi caballo."

The scowl deepened. "No hay agua aqui."

Slade looked toward a windmill beyond the house. "Si no hay agua, porque hay papalote?"

The gun's barrel became more closely aligned with Slade's head. "No hay agua para estranjeros." (No water for foreigners.)

Slade had felt his face grow hot. He eased the Colt out of its holster, thumbed back the hammer—

"Quiero agua para mi caballo, hombre. Pronto!"

His steel-gray eyes bored into the dark eyes of the scarfaced man until the dark eyes wavered and fell, the gunbarrel tilted downward.

"Bueno, senor."

Riding away from the rancho a few minutes later, Slade had turned in the saddle to keep an eye on the Mexican until he was out of range of the flintlock.

The road angled away from the coast, behind a range of low hills. In midafternoon, descending a rough and rocky track into an L-shaped valley, Slade had seen another, more prosperous-looking rancho. There were cornfields and olive groves and vineyards, cattle, sheep, goats and chickens, and in a pole corral several horses—but no big blood-bay Thoroughbred.

Rather than risk another hostile reception, he had skirted the rancho at a safe distance.

Near the south end of the valley he had come to a cluster of roofless, crumbling 'dobe buildings, evidently the remains of an old mission. He'd heard in San Diego how, after the Mexican government secularized the missions thirty-some years ago, rancheros moved in and took over the orchards, vineyards and livestock.

At sunset he had come to a faint trail branching off to the east; so faint Slade hadn't noticed it until Lady, who had had only two drinks from his hat since they left the first rancho, turned into it. Slade tried to rein her back to the road, but the mare, usually so quick to obey, resisted. Looking down at the trail, he had seen hoofprints, including a crimped shoe.

The trail soon dipped into a dry wash. After half a mile the sandy stream bed was broken by a broad slab of volcanic rock. Hollows in the undulating surface held pools of stagnant, scum-covered water.

On the bank nearby had been cigarillo butts, horse droppings and the remains of a fire. Finding the ashes cold, Slade knew the horsethieves were several hours ahead.

He had itched to go on. But it was growing dark, so he had spent the night beside the scummy pools. In the morning he reluctantly filled the canteens from them, straining the algae-and-insect-infested liquid through his shirt, and had followed the trail South.

After about three hours of rolling, slightly rising terrain the trail dipped into a steep, narrow defile, by a series of switchbacks. Nearing the bottom, Slade had seen ahead the arroyo, the small ranch-house and the cactus corral containing the mule and five horses—one of them Prince.

Quickly he had reined Lady around, gone back up the trail, turned off and doubled back to the rim of the arroyo. Picketing the mare in a small, boulder-surrounded enclosure, he had taken up his observation post on the flat rock.

Now the sun was directly overhead, beating down mercilessly on the lifeless landscape. On the stony surface, Slade felt like a hunk· of sausage sizzling on a griddle. Behind him, Lady stood spraddle-legged and hip-shot, head low. In the heat concentrated by the surrounding rocks, sweat had turned her coat almost black.

Down at the forlorn rancho the only thing moving was the windmill, its blades barely revolving in what had fallen off to an all-but-imperceptible breeze.

Slade tensed as the big man and three others, small and dark, came out of the house, followed by a boy of about 16 and an old man with a gimp left leg.

The boy slid aside poles barring the entrance to the cactus corral; the men went inside and caught and saddled the four ponies, leaving Prince and the mule in the corral.

As the pale-haired man swung into the saddle, led the other three toward the rail winding up to the rim of the arroyo, three words flashed through Slade's mind—

He saw me.

Chapter 2

Leaping down from the rock, Slade pulled the picket stake, loosed the reata from Lady's neck, coiled it, jammed his foot in the stirrup, started to swing up into the saddle—

And hung poised for a moment, then let himself drop back to the ground.

What was to be gained by running away?

He had much the best horse. But Lady was jaded from three days on the trail with scant feed and water. He couldn't push her too hard. Couldn't outrun pursuit for more than a few miles, then he'd have to fort up. And if he had to fort up, he sure couldn't find a better spot than where he was right now.

The almost sheer wall of the arroyo behind him looked unclimbable. The clearing was roughly square, ten or twelve yards across, surrounding boulders everywhere more than head high. The only entrance was a narrow passage between two boulders. The side of the square opposite the arroyo was one huge slab of rock, top sloping slightly back toward the clearing.

If he could hold out through the day, maybe come dark he could slip away, sneak down to the ranch and get Prince—head for the border—

A long chance—but a damn sight better than hightailing it and abandoning the colt.

A more immediate problem was Lady. As far as he knew, she'd never heard gunfire. She might panic—try to run away. But to picket her again would cause delay if he had to ride out in a hurry.

He fastened the loop of the reata around the pommel. Then, taking two boxes of shells from a saddle bag, one each for the revolver and the carbine, slinging the remaining full canteen over his shoulder, he climbed up on the rock. Again removing the high-crowned hat, pushing it well back out of sight, he took his position about in the center of the broad slab, using the coiled remainder of the reata as a cushion for his elbows.

He pulled the hammer of the Colt to half cock, turned the cylinder, took a shell from the box of .36 caliber ammo and slid it into the chamber he normally left empty under the hammer. Thinking as he did so, *thank God for that greatest development of the late war, metal cartridges.* Also, thank God he'd taken the time to have the revolver converted at a gunsmith's in Louisville. If he'd had to mess around ramming in powder and ball and putting percussion caps on nipples—

As it was, with the revolver's six shots and the eight .50 caliber rimfire shells in the carbine's magazine he figured he had a good chance to stand off four men indefinitely.

Weapons ready, Slade got out his tobacco pouch and papers, made himself a cigarette, lit it, and checked the terrain.

The ground sloped downward away from the

edge of the arroyo. There were a lot of rocks out there, but those nearby were mostly small. The nearest cover for more than a single man was a big rockpile near where the trail emerged from the arroyo.

There was one potential danger spot. A couple of hundred yards to the west, near the arroyo rim, a huge boulder thrust itself up more than twice as high as the one he was on. But the ground for some distance around the monolith was devoid of rocks or brush—he should be able to keep anyone from getting to it.

Hearing the sound of hoofs on the trail, he stubbed out his cigarette and brought the carbine to his shoulder.

Should he start throwing lead when the first rider appeared?

Maybe the light-haired man hadn't seen him. Maybe the horsethieves had brought Prince down to this remote rancho to hide him, were heading north again to San Diego—or Los Angeles—to find a buyer.

The four riders came up out of the defile, spurred their horses into a trot—a gallop—suddenly swung off the trail to disappear behind the big rockpile.

He'd been seen.

Moments later, another doubt was dispelled.

"Shelbourne," a voice called, "we know yore in there. Come out with yore holster empty and yore hands on yore haid."

No mistaking that harsh, grating Cumberland Mountains twang. It was the voice of Linc Weaver.

The voice that still haunted his nightmares of Fort Delaware. *Move it, Shelbourne—off yore ass, damn you. Get to work you scum. This ain't yore fancy horse farm in Jessamine County, you sneakin', raidin', would-be jailbreakin' reb.*

What the hell was Linc Weaver doing here in the wilds of Baja California?

He'd been to California before the war, Slade remembered. In fact, it had been Linc's account of the Californios' pride in their horseflesh that had given Slade the idea of bringing his Thoroughbreds west. Had he returned to become the leader of a band of border horsethieves?

Slade's thoughts were interrupted by Linc's voice, hollering again from behind the rockpile.

"All right, Shelbourne—I'm countin' to three— then we're gonna blast you outa there."

Slade kept silent. Linc couldn't be sure he was still here. He was bluffing.

"One—"

Besides, the sound of his voice would give them something to shoot at.

Slade's eyes searched the rockpile.

"Two—"

Was that the crown of a hat near one edge of the rockpile? Or just a rounded stone? He shifted the carbine, sighted on the object, but didn't fire. He wasn't going to be caught by the old hat-on-a-stick trick.

"Three!"

Four puffs of smoke blossomed from the rock-pile—none near the hat-crown that must be a rock.

Three shots went high, the fourth slug hit the lip

of the rock, sprayed stone particles in Slade's face and ricocheted whiningly away.

He wiped rock dust and sweat from his eyes, glanced over his shoulder to check Lady. The mare had her ears pricked, but seemed calm.

More shots rang out, hit the rock off to his left. Seconds later another volley was to the right.

"Shelbourne—"

There was a note of doubt in Linc Weaver's voice.

"Come out of there, Shelbourne, or we'll come in after you."

"Come right ahead," Slade muttered through clinched teeth. He nestled the smooth stock of the carbine against his cheek, waiting for the horse-thieves to show themselves.

When two of them rode out from either side of the rockpile a couple of minutes later, rifles in hand, neither of them was Linc.

Slade sighted on the rider to the left; was squeezing the trigger when rock dust again exploded in his face—he flinched, his shot went wild.

Linc and the other man were providing covering fire.

The horsemen, at the sound of Linc's shot, whirled and dashed back toward the rockpile. Before they disappeared Slade got off another shot; saw the man on the left grab his right arm with his left hand and drop his rifle—then he was gone behind the jumble of boulders.

Maybe that lowered the odds. But now they knew for sure he was here.

He pulled the carbine back alongside him, drew out the magazine tube from the muzzle end and fed in a couple of fresh shells.

For a time there was no sound from the rockpile. Probably they were taking care of the man he'd winged. Finally Linc called out—

"All right, Shelbourne—we're gonna get you now. You won't come outa there alive."

No point remaining silent any longer.

"Go to hell, Linc."

For emphasis, Slade sighted on the hat-shaped rock and squeezed off a shot.

The rock flew up and back.

It had been a hat, after all. Not the hat-on-a-stick trick, but the hat-on-a-rock trick.

Well, somebody's hat had a hole in it.

So did somebody's arm. And somebody's rifle lay on the ground fifteen yards from the rockpile. Until a horse leaped out from behind the rocks, its rider, leg hooked over the saddle, hanging from the far side. Swooping low, scooping up the rifle, wheeling the pony and dashing back toward the rockpile.

Slade snapped off a hurried shot, but the pony swerved and disappeared behind the boulders.

Again reloading the carbine, Slade wondered what they'd try next.

In a few minutes he found out.

A man on foot, carrying a rifle, broke away from one side of the rockpile. Slade swung the carbine, but before he could fire, the running man dropped behind a rock.

Only then did he realize another man had broken

from the other side. He swung the carbine that way, but the man disappeared behind a boulder as Slade became aware that slugs were buzzing by his head.

He moved himself back, squirmed sideways, moved forward, raised his head just in time to see the first man come out from behind his rock, scurry forward a few strides, then drop behind another rock.

Slade trained the carbine on the boulder the second man was concealed behind. Too late he glimpsed the first man rise again, advance another few yards.

It was a guessing game, and he was guessing wrong.

Better stop guessing.

He held the carbine centered between the two attackers' positions. When one man darted from behind his rock Slade snapped off three quick shots, not really bothering to aim, but the third kicked up sand under the man's feet as he made a flying leap for safety behind another rock. Quickly Slade swung the carbine to the other man's position, layed a warning shot on that boulder.

He changed position, refilled the carbine's magazine, popped another shot at each man-concealing rock.

He continued these tactics, with frequent position changes to frustrate the covering fire from the rockpile—the wounded man evidently wasn't hurt badly enough to keep him from handling a gun.

The two attackers soon realized they were going

to have two or three slugs buzzing by their heads each time they moved. Then, when one of them left a foot partially in view and Slade knocked the heel off his boot—

Shouts in Spanish between the men and the rockpile. When they moved again it was not forward, but back. When they had regained the shelter of the rockpile—Slade holding his fire to conserve ammunition—Linc called out again—

"If that's the way you want it, Shelbourne, you can sit there and fry in yore own juice."

Trouble was, Slade thought, he didn't have much juice left to fry in. Just the scummy water in one canteen—and that would have to go to Lady.

The thought made him realize how dry he was. His mouth felt like it was stuffed with gun wadding.

That damn sun wasn't helping any. He twisted his head to look up. The glaring globe of molten gold seemed to be stuck right at the zenith. Stubbornly refusing to start that long slide down the western sky that would ultimately bring the cooling relief of evening. And finally, darkness, when he might escape.

Escape.

As his glare-reddened eyes gazed out on the barren landscape to that rockpile behind which waited four men intent on his death, his memory went back through the years to another time— another place.

Chapter 3

The state penitentiary at Columbus, Ohio, in November, 1863.

Lieutenant Slade Shelbourne, 2nd Kentucky Cavalry, CSA, squeezed his shoulders through the snug opening in the cement-and-brick floor and hoisted himself up into the cell. He sprang out of the way as Captain Thomas Hines shoved his green-and-gold carpetbag over the opening and quickly lowered the metal-framed bed onto its swing-away legs on top of the bag.

"Damn near there, Tom," Slade said. "I figure one more day."

"Sure hope so," said Hines, a thin, flap-eared man in his late twenties. "If the army and the prison guards ever make up their minds who is supposed to inspect the cells, we're finished."

As Slade started toward the open cell door, Hines caught his arm.

"Hold it," he said. "Your feet—"

Looking down, Slade saw flecks of damp earth on the cement floor.

"Sorry," he said. "Thought I got it all off. Pretty dark down there, even with the candles."

"Sure," said Hines. He stepped to the door of the cell and glanced both ways along the corridor.

Seeing no guards, he turned back and nodded toward the bed. "Sit."

Hines cleared the soles of Slade's boots carefully with a brush; put the dirt in a cloth sack, which he stuffed into a slit in his mattress.

"Can't dump it back down the hole," he said, "or the next man would bring it back. Should leave some rags down there, I guess, for cleaning shoes. If we can find any someone's not wearing." He chuckled ruefully.

Slade glanced down at the frayed cuffs of his broadcloth shirt, the threadbare knees of his gray twill breeches. They hadn't been in much better condition on that hot July day in Ohio's Beaver Creek Valley when the remnants of General John Hunt Morgan's Confederate raiders had been forced to surrender.

Hard to believe it had been four months since the daring cavalry raid—that had carried the war for the first time into Indiana and Ohio—had ended within sight of the Ohio River, on whose far bank lay comparative safety. Four months of frustration and blighted hopes. Until, finally abandoning dreams of exchange and parole, Morgan and the sixty-some officers the Yankees had confined like common criminals in the state penitentiary—instead of at Johnson's Island military prison near Cincinnati—turned their thoughts to escape.

It had been Hines who made the discovery that gave their escape dreams substance. He noticed that as the fall weather became cold and rainy the cement floor of his cell remained dry. Did this mean, as it did in a book he was reading, Hugo's

Les Miserables, that there was an air passage under his cell?

It did, Hines deduced from skillfully oblique questioning of a grizzled old turnkey named Hevay.

The next morning, while some kept watch in the long corridor in front of the cells, where prisoners were allowed to roam at will during the day, others, using knives smuggled from the dining hall, took turns scraping away at the cement under Hines' bunk. The scrapings, secreted in handkerchiefs, were surreptitiously dumped in the ash pan of the pot-bellied stove at the end of the cellblock. Larger chunks were hidden in mattresses. Whenever one of the lookouts spotted a guard, Hines placed his carpet bag over the growing excavation, lowered his bed and sat on it, reading. It pleased his sense of irony to appear to be reading *Les Miserables*.

When the prisoners selected to do the work—not all were told of the project, though most suspected something was going on in Hines's cell—had laboriously scraped away more than a foot of cement, they hit brick.

After that the work went faster. It was possible to gouge out mortar from between the bricks, and when two layers had been removed, kick the third and last layer through—leaving a gaping hole as the bricks thudded on a dirt floor several feet below.

Slade, who happened to be working at the time, dropped through the hole into a passage about four feet deep, its sides and arched ceiling entirely of brick.

"I knew it," Hines said triumphantly, handing down a candle. Slade explored the passage. It ran the length of the cell block, dead-ending against the stone outer wall of the building.

In a few days mortar had been dug away and enough of the large stone blocks removed to reveal that nothing more formidable than plain dirt lay beyond the wall. The long passage provided plenty of space to accommodate dirt removed in digging the tunnel.

There was only one problem. Which way to dig?

There were no windows at the back of the cells, where beyond the prison yard were inner and outer walls, both reputedly with foundations down to bedrock. No one knew exactly how far it was to the walls, nor what obstacles might be encountered in the yard.

When a first blind attempt was made to tunnel upward, they came up under a coalpile. After this abortive exit was carefully shored up, it was decided nothing more could be done until someone had gotten a look at the yard.

It was General Morgan himself who devised a scheme to accomplish this.

The only windows in the back wall of the cell-block were high up under the roof, above the second tier of cells. A framework of iron posts running from floor to ceiling supported the balcony fronting this upper tier.

In talking with guards, some prisoners had learned that several years earlier a group of con-victs had succeeded in scaling the framework and escaping through skylights.

General Morgan struck up a conversation with a rather thick-witted turnkey named Scott, pointing out that the skylights were still unbarred.

"Aren't you afraid we'll escape the same way?" the general said.

"Why, there isn't a man alive today who could climb up there," Scott said scornfully. "Not even you, General," he added, eyeing Morgan's muscular six-foot-two frame.

"Reserving judgment on myself," the general said, "I'll make you a wager we have a man who can do it."

"And I'll make you a wager you don't," said Scott.

"Captain Taylor!" Morgan called, "Where's Captain Taylor?"—knowing full well that Captain Sam Taylor, carefully briefed on his part in the scheme, was feigning sleep on his cot.

When the small but wiry-muscled captain appeared, yawning and rubbing his eyes, the general told him of the bet. Taylor eyed the scaffolding somewhat dubiously. But when he started to climb, all pretense vanished. Swiftly he swung from bar to bar like a squirrel scampering up a familiar tree, and in scarcely a minute he was at the top, perched under the skylight, putting out a hand as though to open it.

"Bye-bye, Scott," he called down tauntingly.

"Hey, you," the turnkey yelled in alarm, "you get right back down here, right now!"

But Sam Taylor took his time, getting a good look at the prison yard through the upper windows before nimbly descending to the group below.

"Nothing to it," he crowed. "I can get out of here any time I want."

"No you can't," growled Scott. "I'll damn well see to that." And he marched Taylor to his cell and locked the door. Within the hour a work crew entered the cellblock, and by nightfall the skylights were barred.

"Now you can climb up there all you damn want to," Scott jibed at Taylor the next morning as he let him out of his cell. But later in the day, as he convened an informal conference of those involved in the escape plan, General Morgan chuckled—

"I didn't mean it that way, but it served as a good diversion. And now they think they've got the only possible escape route blocked."

He went on to discuss the rough map of the prison yard drawn up by Taylor, and selected the spot where the tunnel should emerge.

Once they knew where they were going, the tunneling went faster—especially after they got the shovel.

A battered, bent and rusty shovel, its handle split, was found, apparently discarded, in the yard the military prisoners marched through to the dining hall. It was sneaked back into the cellblock under a long, loose duster worn by Captain Jack Bennett.

As the digging progressed, so did other preparations.

Calvin Morgan, the general's brother, worked long hours at night braiding rope from bits of cloth torn by the prisoners from their bedding and threadbare clothing. A poker taken from the pot-bellied iron stove that provided the cellblock's only heat was bent double and fastened to one end of the rope, to be used as a grappling hook to scale the walls. Table knives smuggled out of the dining hall were fashioned into crude small-scale Bowie knives. And civilian clothing was obtained through the efforts of Confederate sympathizers outside the prison—ostensibly to replace utterly worn-out uniforms.

These things done and the excavation nearly finished, two decisions remained to be made—who would attempt to escape, and when.

Both subjects were discussed at another informal meeting, the morning after Slade had emerged from the hole in Hines's cell with word the tunnel was almost completed.

Six of them lounged in the corridor in front of Captain Bennett's cell, apparently casually, but keeping a sharp eye out for the military guards. The army guarded the prisoners during the day, penitentiary personnel at night. This divided responsibility was the reason, as Hines had mentioned to Slade, neither group had made a thorough inspection of the cells for several weeks.

General Morgan, managing to look militarily erect while lounging againstthe stone-block outer wall, brushed a knuckle across his new mustache—Merion, the warden, had submitted him to the indignity of a shave and convict haircut when they arrived.

"You say we're almost through?" the general asked Slade.

"Very close, sir." Slade felt awed and honored —he was the youngest and most junior officer in the group. The others were the general's brother and Captain Hines, Taylor and Bennett. But Slade's rise had been rapid since he saddled one of Shelbourne Farm's few remaining Thoroughbreds and rode over to Richmond, Kentucky, in July of '62 to join Morgan's forces, then withdrawing from an earlier raid. He had distinguished himself particularly the following winter in Morgan's Christmas raid, had been thawed from that freezing New Year's ride back into Tennessee by the general's personal commendation. Soon afterwards he had been named adjutant of the 2nd Kentucky, commanded by Major T.C. Webber— now a fellow prisoner at the penitentiary.

"Well," said John Morgan, sweeping the group with his penetrating glance, "it's time we decided who's going."

It had been obvious from the start that a mass breakout was impossible. Such a large number of men leaving the area of the penitentiary would be bound to attract attention—early discovery—a dragnet. But if only a handful went, and split up in different directions—

Also, since the escape would have to be made at night, after the prisoners were locked in their individual cells, only those on the ground floor could go—the plan being to remove the bricks and all but a thin layer of cement from the passage below the cells before the breakout.

This posed a major problem. Everyone agreed that General Morgan must escape, to form a new band of raiders to carry on the Confederate cause. But the general's cell was on the second tier.

Calvin Morgan, who had a lower cell, provided the solution.

"We'll trade places before lockup," he said to his brother. "We're built enough alike—if the turnkey doesn't see our faces—"

The general gave his brother a long, level look. "Thanks, Callie. Good idea. All right—who else?"

It was quickly decided that Hines, Taylor, Bennett and Captain L.D. Hockersmith of the 10th Cavalry, who had been one of the principal organizers of the escape effort, would go.

"One or two more," said the general.

"How about Major Webber?" Hines suggested.

"I don't know," said Taylor. "He's been pretty sick—hasn't been right since the warden had him put in solitary—down in the hole."

"Why don't you put it to him?" suggested General Morgan.

Taylor left, returned in a couple of minutes shaking his head.

"Says he's been spending half his time on the slop bucket—too weak to make it over the hills, let alone get back to our lines."

John Morgan shook his head. "Too bad—it'd be nice to have somebody from the old Second Cav."

The Second Kentucky Cavalry had evolved from the contingent of Lexington Rifles that Morgan had led to join the Confederate forces in September of '61. Slade became aware that the general was looking at him, the knuckle again stroking his mustache.

"How about you, Shelbourne? Will you represent the Second?"

Slade felt his cheeks growing hot. Though he had been one of the most enthusiastic workers in the escape effort, he had really never considered the possibility he might be chosen to make the attempt. There were so many more experienced officers. Why, he was only a few months past his nineteenth birthday. The mustache growing out again above his upper lip had never been more than a wispy imitation of a true cavalryman's brush.

"I—I would be honored, sir."

John Morgan nodded. "Very good. Well, would anyone like to suggest someone else?"

After some moments of silence, when it seemed no one else was going to speak, Slade cleared his throat. The general's gaze returned to him.

"Yes, Shelbourne?"

"I was thinking, sir—Linc—uh—Lieutenant Weaver—the scout. He grew up in eastern Kentucky, knows all the gaps through the Cumberlands—"

General Morgan's rather heavy, low-set eyebrows drew together slightly.

"Weaver? Hasn't been with us long, has he?"

"No, sir," Slade admitted. "Only since May—about six weeks before we started across the river. But—"

The general's upraised hand halted him. He looked at Taylor, kin of Zachary Taylor and Morgan's most trusted scout.

"What do you know of him, Sam?"

"Good man, General. Mountain raised, and he's been west—all the way to California—picked up a lot of tricks from the mountain men and Indians along the way."

Morgan continued to look at him, eyes intent. "But can we trust him?"

Taylor shrugged. Then Slade found himself saying—

"I'll vouch for him, sir. I've known him for a long time—since I was a boy."

Remembering that first trip east with his father as a youth of thirteen. Taking a band of Shelbourne Farm colts through the Cumberlands to be sold in Virginia and the Carolinas. Linc Weaver, then nineteen, oldest of ten kids trying to subsist with their parents on a rock-studded one-mule farm near Pound Gap, making the rest of the trip with them, working for two-bits a day and food.

John Morgan's eyes twinkled.

"Known him a long time, have you? Well, all right, if you vouch for him, Weaver can go. Now," —he looked at Hines—"how soon can we be ready?"

When Hines said two days, three at the most, the general continued—

"Let's see—this is Thursday—to be safe, let's say Monday."

But the next morning circumstances dictated a sudden change of plans. Word reached them through the prison grapevine that a new military commander had been appointed for Columbus.

"Sure as Christmas the first thing he'll do is inspect the penitentiary," John Morgan told a hastily-called meeting of the would-be escapees. "Tom," he said to Hines, "can we possibly be ready by tonight?"

Captain Hines's narrow chin firmed, thrust forward—

"We will be, General."

That night Slade lay on his bunk in the dark. Heard, at last, the metallic clang of the cellblock door as the guard arrived to make his regular midnight inspection. The break was to be immediately after midnight—General Morgan and Hines wanted to take the one a.m. train out of Columbus for Cincinnati. The others were going divergent ways—Slade and Linc Weaver southeast because of the mountaineer's knowledge of the Kentucky-Virginia border region.

It had given Slade a good feeling to tell Linc he was being included in the escape attempt. It was paying a debt, in a way. A scene flashed through his mind—a boy tossed by a panicky colt into a swift-flowing mountain torrent. Linc flinging a rope, the end just reaching Slade's clutching hands.

Listening, Slade heard the guard's footsteps making gritty-scratchy sounds on the cement floor. The prisoners had scattered coal dust to give warning of a surprise approach—a pet trick of Scott's.

The footsteps came nearer, then as light from an upheld lantern washed his cell, Slade forced himself to imitate the deep, even breathing of sleep.

The light faded as the footsteps went on down the corridor to the end, returned. Slowly the footsteps ascended the metal stairway to the second tier, moved along the balcony, came back, down the stairs again. At last the cellblock door clanged shut, the key turned in the lock.

Slade waited in the dark for what seemed hours but was probably only about five minutes before he heard two thumps on the floor beneath his bed: Tom Hines, in the passage below, giving the signal for the break to begin.

Quickly he rolled off the cot, lifted it up against the wall and stamped on the floor. The thin layer of remaining cement cracked, crumbled, fell through.

Slade let the bed down again and put his threadbare bundled-up prison garb—he was wearing dark-colored civilian trousers and coat—under the blanket, lumped up to look like a human figure.

Catching up a small bundle of personal things wrapped in a spare shirt, clutching his makeshift Bowie knife, Slade squirmed under the bed through the hole in the floor and dropped into the passage below.

Hines, General Morgan and Tayler were already there; dim outlines in the light of a single candle, shrouded by dust from the fallen concrete. In moments they were joined by Bennett, Hockersmith, and finally, Linc Weaver.

They hurried up to the end of the passage, where Hines and Taylor disappeared, on hands and knees, into the three-foot diameter tunnel. Taylor carried another lighted candle, Hines the shovel, to break through the last thin layer of dirt.

In three or four minutes Taylor was back, shoving a boxfull of damp dirt in front of him.

"Great news," he whispered. "It's raining!"

"Thank God!" breathed John Morgan.

Rain would keep the dogs, who were turned

loose each night in the prison yards, in their kennels, and the guards under cover and near fires.

One by one the others crawled into the tunnel until only Slade and Linc Weaver were left. Slade motioned for Linc to go ahead, but the big man shook his head.

"You first," he whispered.

Slade dropped to his knees and entered the dank, dark opening. A very faint light showed up ahead from the carefully shielded candles. Between them bulked the forms of his fellow escapees, each almost filling the passage.

After he had gone a little way Slade paused, looked back over his shoulder.

What he saw confirmed what his ears had already told him—the absence of slithering sounds from behind to go with those ahead—

Linc Weaver wasn't following.

For a moment Slade could see Linc's legs dimly outlined at the end of the passage, then they moved away.

As fast as he could, Slade backed out of the tunnel.

Rising, turning, he saw Linc, one cupped hand shielding a small candle, scuttling away down the brick-walled passage.

"Linc!" Slade hissed.

Linc stopped, turned.

"Where are you going, Linc?" Slade said in a hoarse whisper. "What's the matter—did you forget something?"

Linc's light blue eyes shifted behind the flickering candle, darted from one wall of the passage to the other, glanced upward.

"No—no, I ain't forgot nothin'."

"Then come on, man. We can't lose any time. Hurry!"

Slade stepped forward to take Linc's arm, start him back toward the tunnel. But Linc stepped back, evaded his grasp.

"No—don't touch me—keep yore hands off me, Shelbourne."

As Slade reached for him again, Linc shrank away.

"No! Don't—"

It was only as his hand caught the glint of candlelight on metal that Slade realized his left hand, with which he was trying to grab Linc, still held the Bowie. Quickly he dropped the hand to his side.

"Hell, Linc, I wasn't going to cut you. But come on, we've got to go."

Linc took another step away.

"No. I ain't goin'."

As Linc's eyes again shifted upward, Slade realized they stood under the opening to one of the cells.

Suspicion flooded his mind—suspicion instantly confirmed by what he saw in the other's eyes.

Linc Weaver was going to betray them—at that moment was opening his mouth to yell.

Slade's right fist lashed out, smashed into the big man's mouth. Smashed the sound back down his throat, so all that came out was a smothered grunt. Smashed him backward—reeling—falling—

Pain throbbing in the hand that had struck the

blow, Slade lunged forward, stumbled over Linc's prostrate form. Throwing out his hands to break his fall, he lost the knife. Groping for it on the dirt floor, his hands encountered Linc's body.

The big man was trying to rise. Slade, on his knees, swung for where Linc's head should be—this time with his left. His fist crashed against a whiskery jaw.

Then he was astride the other, both fists hurting, listening to Linc's heavy breathing—waiting for him to move. The form under Slade stirred slightly. At the same time dim light glowed again in the passage. Soft footsteps approached from the direction of the tunnel.

"Shelbourne—what the hell's going on here?"

Turning his head, Slade saw Sam Taylor coming toward him, holding a candle.

"He was going to turn us in."

The bushy brows above Taylor's dark eyes drew together.

"The hell he was!"

Taylor stooped, picked up Slade's knife from the floor, stepped forward and thrust it into his hand.

"Kill the bastard," he said. "Slit his squawkin' throat."

Slade, knife poised, looked down on the face with its pale yellow straggly mustache and beard. The blue eyes were open, sweat beads popping out on the prison-pallid forehead.

Staring into those eyes, Slade felt sweat forming on his own brow—cold sweat. Suddenly in those eyes he seemed to glimpse a rope snaking out over white-swirling water.

And he knew he couldn't kill Linc Weaver. Not then—not that way. Not unless there was no other choice.

But if they left him, Linc would give the alarm. The escape would be thwarted before General Morgan and the others got over the wall. Even if they tied Linc up and gagged him, he'd eventually get loose. They were counting on the break not being discovered until the turnkey made his regular appearance at six. By then the train the General and Tom Hines planned to take would be in Cincinnati, the others would be well started on their various escape routes.

No—Linc Weaver had to be kept silent. Slade knew what he had to do.

"You go on," he said to Taylor without taking his eyes from Linc's face. "I'll stay here and make sure he doesn't give the alarm. If he so much as tries to squeak, I'll kill him."

As he spoke, his eyes burned the message into Linc's, and from the look reflected there he knew Linc believed him.

"Why that way?" Taylor said, stepping closer. "Why not just cut his throat. It's obvious he's a damn Yankee spy—been spyin' on us all along. We're lucky he didn't squawk before—probably wanted to wait and have us caught in the act."

"Be that as it may," Slade said, "I won't kill him."

"Good lord, man—why not?"

"I've got my reasons. A debt—"

"It'll go hard with you," Taylor warned. "The escape—they'll be mad as hell. At the least, solitary —maybe they'll hang you—"

Slade shook his head. "A chance I have to take. You go on—quick. Just get me the other candle—it's around here somewhere—light it."

Within seconds Sam Taylor had complied with that request and cat-footed off down the passage, disappeared into the tunnel.

Slade, holding the knife ready, rose carefully to a crouch, backed away a step and motioned for Linc to move to the wall of the passage. When the big man was in a sitting position on one side, Slade lowered himself to squat against the other wall, weight forward, ready to spring at the slightest sign Linc was going to call out.

They stayed that way, the candle flickering as a cool, moist draft moved down the passage from the open escape tunnel. From time to time Slade shifted position, rising to his feet occasionally to be sure his muscles didn't cramp.

They said nothing. Once Linc moved his lips as though to speak—instantly Slade was on him, the roughly honed knife blade at his throat.

Finally the candle hissed, guttered and died—but the dim gray of dawn filtered down through the holes in seven cell floors. Not much later, the silence was broken by a loud clanging noise above, the turnkey beating the iron stove with a poker, the regular wakeup signal.

Only then, knowing discovery would come in moments, did Slade speak.

"Why, Linc?" he asked. "Why?"

Chapter 4

The sun had reluctantly inched halfway down the western sky, but it was hotter than ever.

Behind him Slade heard Lady's breath coming long, slow and hard. Time to use the last of the water.

He slipped down off the rock, emptied the canteen into his hat and let Lady drink. Taking a rag from a saddlebag he sponged out the inside of the hat, put the rag in his mouth and sucked on it as he climbed back up on the rock.

The rag went dry in his mouth; noticing it matched the sandy-gray of the surrounding boulders, he draped it over his head, partly as camouflage, partly to protect the sun-scorched back of his neck.

In a few minutes the rag was so dry it crinkled like paper when he raised his head slightly to squint out over the barren landscape at the rockpile behind which four men waited to kill him.

They hadn't been trying very hard in the last three hours. Only an occasional shot—reminders of their presence rather than serious attempts to hit him. Still, Slade shifted his position from time to time. He didn't return their fire. Let them wonder whether he was still here or had somehow escaped.

When he heard thudding hoofbeats, saw one of the dark men galloping toward the trail into the arroyo, he still didn't shoot. Then he had second thoughts. Three-to-one is better odds than four-to-one. Well, it would be easy enough to pick that rider off when he came up out of the arroyo again.

Nearly another hour dragged by before the sound of hoofs on the rocky trail alerted Slade to the rider's return. He swung the carbine toward the top of the defile, sighted on the emerging horseman —abruptly raised his head from the stock—

There was not one horseman, but two. And the nearest rider, screening the other, wasn't a horseman, on two counts.

First, this horseman's mount was a mule. The mule that had been left in the corral with Prince when Linc and his three men had ridden up to attack Slade.

Second, as evidenced by the long, full sweep of bright orange material hanging from saddle to stirrup, this wasn't a horseman—it was a horse-woman. Above the skirt was a small, erect, white-shirted figure, balancing a large kettle on the saddlehorn.

Slade swore.

Linc Weaver not only had a woman to screen the returning horsethief, she was bringing them their dinner.

As dry as his mouth was, Slade thought he detected a slight seepage of saliva as he wondered what was in the kettle.

He wasn't long in doubt.

"Ho, Shelbourne," Linc called, "how'd you

like some pasole? Real juicy—mighty tasty.''

Slade recalled sampling the stew-like concoction of hominy, pork and spices at Don Ricardo Castillo's house in San Diego.

''It is not stylish food,'' Juana Castillo had told him, white teeth flashing in a smile. ''Papa says it is fit only for campesinos—country people. But I like it—don't you?''

Slade had agreed. He would have agreed with almost anything Don Ricardo's beautiful 16-year-old daughter said.

Linc Weaver's voice broke into his memory, his nasal twang a violent contrast to Juana Castillo's lilting, Spanish-flavored tones.

''We got us some wine over hyar, too, Shelbourne. Sweet 'n cool—been hangin' in the well. Bet you'd like some.''

Slade fought down the desire to tell Linc where he could go and what he could do when he got there. Damned if he'd give him the satisfaction.

Considerably later, with a sudden drumming of hoofs the mule burst out from behind the rockpile, heading full gallop toward the trail. The rider was bent low over the mule's neck, kettle dangling from right hand, orange skirt flapping in the wind—and as the skirt flared high Slade saw that the legs under it were encased in men's trousers. At the same instant the mule's rider let out a high, shrill, but definitely unfeminine yell.

''Hee-yah—abajo los yanquis!''

Slade snapped off two shots before the mule disappeared into the defile. Both missed. In reply, a volley came from the rockpile; slugs splattered on the rock and whined away.

Seething, Slade fed cartridges into the carbine's magazine. Linc had tricked him. The mule's rider must have been the youth he'd seen earlier down at the rancho.

But maybe it was just as well he'd missed. Shooting kids wasn't much better than shooting women. He recalled from Morgan's raids how many of the dead—on both sides—had been boys younger than himself.

But those four behind the rockpile weren't kids. How Slade wished he could get Linc Weaver in his sights!

And then, when the sun had dipped considerably lower, hanging not far above the coastal hills, he was looking down the barrel of the carbine at Linc —but not squeezing the trigger.

It began with a flash of white waving on a stick above the rockpile.

"Let's talk, Shelbourne," Linc hollered. "Maybe we can make a deal."

Slade suspected a trick. But if there was some way out of this—

He looked back at Lady. Heat and thirst were harder on the mare than they were on him. She'd never make it through another of these scorching Baja days without water.

"What's your deal, Linc?"

"Ah'm tired a hollerin'," Linc yelled back. "Ah'll come over thar an' talk."

"You'll come on foot then," Slade called back. "And unarmed."

After a pause, Linc yelled, "T'hell with that,"

and rode out around one side of the rockpile, rifle in the crook of his arm.

"Careful, Linc," Slade warned as the big man walked his horse slowly forward. "Any of your friends try anything—you get it first."

Linc didn't reply. When he was about twenty-five yards away Slade, the carbine sighted on the middle of his chest, said sharply—

"That's close enough."

Linc reined his mount to a halt.

"All right," Slade bit out, "speak your piece."

"Ah'd shore like to see you daid, Shelbourne," Linc said. "Ah'd like to see you die slow an' painful out here under that sun. But ah've got other things to do. Other fish to fry." He permitted himself a dry chuckle. "So ah'll let you ride out alive."

"What's the catch, Linc?"

Long yellow hair swayed bulky shoulders as Linc shook his head.

"No catch. You gave me my life once. Now ah'm givin' you yores. Jes' git on yore horse and ride out. But keep goin'. Ah'll have someone watchin'."

So that's it, Slade thought. Someone watching—to put a bullet in my back.

Linc might have read his mind—

"Jes' watchin'. My man won't hurt you, long as you ride north. You can even keep yore handgun. Course we'll take the carbine."

Slade was tempted. With his Colt, he could lay a trap for the man Linc assigned to follow him, kill him and double back.

But meantime, where would Linc be off to—with Prince?

No, it was a bad proposition on two counts. First, there was the chance he could get away after dark and rescue Prince. Second, a man would be seven kinds of fool, after what had happened at the Columbus Penitentiary, to trust Linc Weaver.

"No deal, Linc," he said finally. "I don't leave here without my colt."

Linc shook his head.

"I keep the colt, Shelbourne."

"No deal, Linc," Slade repeated, adding, with a jerk of the gun barrel. "On your way."

Linc shrugged. Rifle still held casually in the crook of his arm, he reined his horse around and walked him back toward the rockpile.

Watching his receding back, Slade was touched by a vestige of the admiration he had felt for Linc Weaver when he'd first known him. The admiration of a youth for a young man. A big, easy-going young man already versed in the ways of the wild, an accomplished hunter, reader of sign, handler of stock—

How, Slade wondered, had that man become a spy and a betrayer and now at last a horsethief?

And what was the purpose behind that offer to let him go? Did Linc really have other fish to fry? Was it simply a ruse to lure Slade out of his rock fort and gun him down? Or did Linc have some other scheme?

The sun had sunk to a point where it hung just above that craggy monolith off to his left. A faint breeze had come up, but the air it moved languidly across the rock he lay on was still supercharged with heat from the baking desert.

But the descending sun held hope. When it set, it would turn cooler. Then it would be only a matter of waiting until after dark, when he could try to escape.

He started making plans. He'd muffle Lady's hoofs with pads cut from his blanket—do the same for his boots. Leave saddle and bridle behind to avoid jingling bit and squeaking leather. He could handle the mare with a halter, ride bareback. Once they got clear of Linc and his men, he'd make a big circuit, come back along the arroyo rim, look for another way down so he could get Prince—

His thoughts were abruptly broken off by an outburst of firing from the rockpile. One flurry of shots, seconds later another. Splintered and powdered stone flew up in his face as slugs whistled off in scattered directions.

Slade squirmed hurriedly backward, raised himself on knees and elbows and started to scrabble to his right.

The movement saved his life.

The slug that tore through the fleshy part of his left upper arm seared across his chest instead of blasting through his ribs to his heart.

And as he rolled onto his side, raised the carbine to his shoulder with his right arm, Slade discovered the purpose of Linc's recent parley.

On top of that huge tower of rock to the west, outlined in sharp silhouette against the huge orange ball that seemed to be perched on top of the monolith, was a human figure.

Squinting into the all-but-blinding glare, Slade aimed the carbine and squeezed the trigger just as bright yellow flashed against the sun's deep orange.

Disregarding another spray of stone-splinters as the bullet struck inches from his face, Slade fired again—and saw the figure on the rock whirl—stagger—and then plunge out from the monolith and down—down into the arroyo.

Turning, squirming forward, dragging his numb left arm, Slade looked toward the rockpile. Three riders were coming hell-bent toward him. He triggered the carbine. One of the riders—not big enough to be Linc—swayed in his saddle, leaned forward, clutching his mount's neck. The horse veered away, disappeared down the defile.

Slade fired two more shots. The other riders—Linc and a smaller man—peeled away and retreated at a gallop, took cover again behind the rockpile.

Slade refilled the carbine's magazine—he had better than half a box of shells left. Then he slowly and painfully cut away the sleeve of his shirt to examine the wound in his arm.

He found he could move the arm—slowly and with great effort—so the bullet must have gone through without hitting bone. The muscle was undoubtedly pretty badly torn up, but at least there was no slug in there to dig for.

He wrapped the rag he'd had around his head tightly around the arm, then bound the cutoff shirt sleeve also around the wound.

Trying to ignore the slow, moist seep of blood

from the wound under the bandages, he returned his attention to the rockpile.

The odds were down to two-to-one. He wondered how badly the man was hurt whose mount had taken him down into the arroyo. Seriously enough, he hoped, to keep him out of further action.

Now he knew why Slade had come out to talk—to distract Slade so one of Linc's men could sneak away from the rockpile and work his way to that high rock on the arroyo's rim. But Linc had made his plan a little too complicated. The barrage of fire from the rockpile had evidently been meant to keep Slade occupied, prevent him from spotting the man on the rock. Instead, it had alarmed him into moving just at the critical moment.

He looked again toward the monolith.

The sun had disappeared, but a brilliant glow lighted the sky above the low coastal hills. The light spread until it covered almost half the sky, then gradually decreased in intensity—faded to pale gold, almost the color of Linc Weaver's hair—then to silver—darker gray—darkish blue-gray—

What was going on behind the rockpile? What kind of scheme would Linc cook up next?

Hearing a sound behind him, Slade jerked around. Had someone sneaked up to take him from the rear?

It was only Lady, tugging at a sparse wisp of shrub growing from a small crevice between two boulders.

"Easy girl," Slade muttered. "It won't be long now."

To the east, stars were showing. The sky was darkening overhead. A faint glow remained in the west, outlining rocks, brush and cactus between Slade and the now indistinct jumble of the rock-pile. He strained his eyes to detect the least hint of movement.

The slight breeze had died, adding to the stillness. It was still hot—the daylong heat of the sun was radiating from earth and rocks.

Now, he told himself finally. *Now's the time.* He started to inch backward slowly. The wounded arm had stiffened up and was hurting now—a deep, throbbing hurt.

In spite of the pain, and the slippery-slick pool of blood his bare forearm encountered as he moved, he continued to crawl backward, started to turn—

And stopped—stared in amazement—

The sky to the east, above the distant mountains, was aglow with silvery light. As he watched, the light grew brighter; expanded to cover a larger and larger segment of the sky.

The moon. He'd entirely forgotten the moon.

Four nights ago, when Linc and his men had stolen Prince, the moon had been nearly full. Now it would be a day or two past full.

When the moon topped the hills, it would be almost as bright as day.

So much for his hope of escaping in the dark.

What should he do? Mount Lady and make a break for it now, in the near-dark?

But already it was too late. A gleaming silver disk was climbing above the mountains, and Linc

Weaver's voice called from the rockpile—

"Gonna be a nice bright night, Shelbourne. Good night fer shootin' rebs."

"Good night for shootin' skalawags," Slade yelled back, using the term southerners applied to those who had turned against their cause.

Linc's scornful laugh floated back through the moonlight.

"Come out of there any time you feel like dyin', Shelbourne. We'll jes' be a-settin' here waitin'. As fer that skalywag stuff—remember what I tol' you on the train."

Slade remembered—

What Linc had told him on the train was as much answer as he'd ever gotten to the question he'd asked down in the passage under the Columbus Penitentiary cellblock—why Linc had tried to betray his escaping fellow prisoners.

It hadn't been an immediate answer, because before Linc could speak—if he was going to speak—the old turnkey, Scott, stuck his head down through the cell-floor hole and yelled—

"What the hell's goin' on here?"

Slade never had gotten an answer in so many words. The closest he'd come was a few days later during the long train ride from Columbus to Fort Delaware.

"We'll damn well send Lt. Shelbourne where he won't cause us any more trouble," Warden Merion had said bitterly.

And Linc, to his obvious disgust, had been detailed to guard Slade—handcuffed and leg-shackled—during the trip and thereafter at Fort Delaware, evidently as punishment for having let General Morgan and the others escape.

It wasn't until long after that Slade learned of the flight of Morgan and Tom Hines—the general, in a fine display of bravado, had sat beside a Union officer on the train to Cincinnati—and the perilous journey through enemy territory in Kentucky and Tennessee to eventual safety behind the Confederate lines.

Linc, sullen and taciturn during the entire trip, mellowed somewhat on the evening of the second day, after a portly and well-dressed civilian sent him—now uniformed in Union blue—a bottle of wine in the dining car.

Back in their regular seats it was Linc, lighting a cigar also supplied by the civilian, who opened the subject.

"You know," he said, "t'other night you coulda killed me and got away—but you didn't. I been wonderin' why. You told that Taylor fella you owed me—"

"Don't you remember?" Slade said. "You threw me a rope once."

"Oh—that." Linc stared at something across the aisle. "That was—well—jes' the natural thing to do."

He took a puff on his cigar, looked back at Slade.

"I reckon that makes us even."

"Reckon it does," said Slade. "But I've been wondering. Why did you do it, Linc? Was Sam Taylor right? Were you spying on us all along?"

Linc's face flushed—

"I don' like talk of spyin', Shelbourne. Who's Taylor to be callin' people spies? He calls hisself a scout—but what's he doin' but spyin'? I jes' did a better job, is all. Got myself right in with yore outfit. After we got captured they wanted some 'un inside to keep an eye on yore Genril Morgan, he bein' such a slippery snake. So I did it. An' I'd-a caught him in the act—he'd-a been shot tryin' to escape—if you'd jes' kep' goin' up that tunnel."

For a moment Slade felt furious, wanted to throw himself on Linc Weaver, handcuffs, shackles and all. But he controlled his anger and asked once more—

"But why, Linc?"

Linc looked away again, the skin under his yellow whiskers becoming purple.

"It's a war, ain't it? A man's got a right to pick his own side, don't he? The side that'll do him most good?"

He threw the half-smoked cigar angrily to the floor and ground it under his boot heel. Slade realized the conversation was at an end.

Not long after the moon rose, bathing the desert landscape with a silver sheen, a new breeze sprang up from the east. At first, like the earlier northwesterly breeze, it carried with it the warmth of sunbaked ground. But as the night wore on it became cooler. At first Slade found the coolness a welcome relief. But later, as the breeze grew stronger, it carried cold air from the distant mountains, and as the moon neared the zenith, he found himself trembling from the chill.

The wind blew harder, kicking up wispy sand-swirls around the rocks and straggly brush, and blew colder. Shivering, Slade finally crawled painfully down from the rock—his arm was very stiff now, and aching—got his blanket and took it back up on the rock with him. It helped for a little while, but soon the cold wind seemed to blow right through the blanket, and he started to shake again.

Then he was no longer cold, but hot, and his head started to ache, until he didn't know which ached worse, his head or his arm. His head was dry and aching and hot, but at the same time he was shaking. At intervals the trembling became violent paroxysms shaking his entire body—legs jerking—teeth chattering—

He should get down from the rock, walk around, get the circulation going. But he couldn't. Had to stay up here, watching—

Yet now his vision began to blur. The moonlit desert seemed to come and go—grow hazy, indistinct—roll in billowing waves like a silver sea—

He stuck his finger in his mouth and bit it—hard.

Things cleared up for awhile.

Then they got hazy again.

He bit his finger again—not the same finger.

I'll be all right, he thought grimly, until I run out of fingers.

He was on the first finger of his left hand—that really jarred him, the pain seemed to set off a bomb in the wound in his upper arm—when he saw the glint of moonlight on metal near one end of the rockpile. Saw it for just an instant, then it disappeared.

He squinted—concentrated—

There it was again.

Slowly he lined up the carbine. Let's see now, Linc had carried the rifle in his right arm, so sight a little to the left—no, to the right, it was backwards —no—yes—which—

He bit the second finger of his left hand, put the hand back to the barrel of the carbine, sighted, squeezed the trigger—

There was a yell over by the rockpile, then a low, monotonous cursing—in English.

He fired again—the cursing stopped. Had he killed Linc?

No. Linc's voice, strong and clear, called—

"Good try, Shelbourne. But you jes' winged me. Jes' a scratch. We're still here waitin' fer you."

The hell with waiting, Slade told himself. *I'm going out there and take it to 'em.*

First, reload the carbine. He fumbled for the box of cartridges. How many shots had he fired? Two? He picked up one cartridge. Trying to pick up the second, he dropped the first. His fingers felt thick, like sausage links. Shouldn't have bitten them so hard. The thought made his fingers hurt. His arm hurt. His head. The desert was becoming enveloped in fog, first moonlight silver, then darkening, until an impenetrable black cloud closed in on him.

He was awakened by a buzzing in his ears.

Still shivering—and still hot. Especially hot on

his right side. His head was turned that way—he opened his eyes. The glare of the sun blinded him.

By tremendous effort, he raised his head, got his elbows under him.

The buzzing grew louder. Huge flies swarmed on the sodden rags around his arm and the pool of blood on the rock.

He looked across the sun-shimmering desert to the rockpile.

Were they still out there?

What did it matter? He had to get out of here—now. Get out of here or die.

He turned and painfully inched his way across the rock. Lady stood alongside a boulder, partly shaded from the sun's heat. The reata was still looped around the pommel, and to his surprise, the loose end was still on the rock. He grasped it, tugged—

Lady walked over to stand beside the rock.

He pulled himself to a sitting position—exposed, now, to anyone standing on the rockpile. Sat still, expecting a slug to smash into his back. When nothing happened, he dangled his legs over the edge of the rock, got a toe in a stirrup. Leaned forward, grabbed the horn with both hands—wincing as pain stabbed through his left arm—transferred his weight to the saddle.

He looked around—something was missing. Saw his hat, the carbine, boxes of cartridges, still on the rock beside the pool of blood. Nearby, the rumpled blanket.

Couldn't do anything about that now.

He pulled the Colt from its holster, tried to

thumb back the hammer, found it was too weak. The effort made his vision dim—the earth tilted up toward him—

The saddlehorn jabbed into his middle. He realized the hair in his face was Lady's mane. He clung to her neck with his right arm—his left hanging limp.

"Get us out of here, girl," a far-away voice said.

He felt the mare step out.

Chapter 5

Heat—
Damp, soggy, humid—
Fort Delaware was on an island in the river. An island, most of which was below the level of the river at high water, the water held back by dikes. On each bank of the river was swampy marshland.

Saturation humidity all during the long, hot summer.

Rare breezes slowly moving miasmic superheated fetid air of the swamps across the island.

Nights, Slade lay on his bunk naked except for a tattered rag across his middle. Someone had told him that a cloth across the middle would prevent cramps and dysentery. It wasn't true; he had them all the time.

He lay drenched in sweat that caused sores on his body and itching heat rash, turning and tossing.

Days, his ragged blue shirt and trousers were permanently sodden with sweat and condensation of the saturated air.

Cold—
There seemed no spring or fall in this country. Only summer and winter. Hot and cold.

Chilling days—sleeting rain—it seldom truly snowed here on the Delaware. But the damp air established a deep-bone chill that lasted from the time the heat broke in the fall until it suddenly clamped down again after the final late spring storm, which came on the wings of ripping north winds that blasted sheets of granular ice across the island.

To counter the cold—a single coal stove in each shed. One hundred and ten men, give or take a few depending on how many had been hauled off to the hospital that day, crowded around it, warmed as much by mutual body heat as by the stove.

With a single thin blanket as shield against the cold, Slade curled up in a knot on his bunk at night, arms wrapped around knees, shivering, closing his eyes but seemingly never able to escape into sleep.

The first winter was bad enough, though he'd been in fairly good condition when he arrived from Columbus. But the second winter, with almost all the flesh gone off his body, skin hanging on bones, hollow cheeked, spindly flanked, belly sunk in under the bony overhang of his rib cage—the second winter was a frigid hell.

Hunger—

Continually on the thin edge of starvation.

A few hardtack biscuits a day, and a piece of meat. Usually rancid, sometimes wormy, bacon—a chunk about the size of a small hen's egg. Sometimes biscuits ran short. Sometimes there was no meat. "Went bad—can't get more 'til next week," the mess servers said callously.

Some prisoners supplemented these meager rations by hunting rats, with which the island abounded. Not the ordinary city rat, or shipboard rat, but a water rat that made its home in burrows honeycombing the dank, dark, moist soil.

Men with clubs would sit patiently beside a burrow for hours, until a rat appeared, which they promptly brained and carried off to the fire or stewpot.

Slade couldn't eat rat.

"Why it's prime," said one of the rat-devotees, a grizzle-bearded captain. "Tender and tasty as rabbit or chicken. A rat is really a very clean, neat animal, you know. Not like a pig. Filthy habits, pigs—but you eat pork. Why not rat?"

Why not rat? Simple prejudice. He'd always heard rats were dirty scavengers. Besides, they carried plague. He'd rather starve—and damn near did.

Thirst—

Water from the tanks at best was foul smelling, brackish, filled with sediment and living organisms you tried to leave squirming and wiggling in the bottom of your cup—knowing full well that many again passed down your throat.

The tanks were barely adequate to supply the prisoner population during rainy weather. In dry seasons they had to be replenished daily from a small water boat that was supposed to go far enough up the creek to get fresh water. But the boat crew didn't have to drink that water, so they didn't go above tidewater, but instead brought back briny water. When dumped through hose pipes into the tanks this stirred up the contents of waggletails, worms, dead leaves, even dead—and live—fish.

Briny water that made all who drank it thirst for more—and more—and more—

And as Slade drank the salty water it poured off his body in salty sweat as he labored with the prison's chain gang.

Work—

Lieutenant Slade Shelbourne had been speechless with shock and outrage that first day at Fort Delaware when, under Linc Weaver's supervisory eye, he was made to strip off the clothing he'd worn from Columbus and don an old pair of Union Army government issue pants, join the work gang of criminals from the Yankee army under sentence for the most noxious of crimes—murderers—deserters—thieves—perverts—

This crew did all the hardest and dirtiest work of the prison. Filling old latrines and digging new ones, garbage detail, burial detail—and hauling stones and timbers for building projects. In a masterpiece of irony, this gang of cutthroats and worse hauled all the material that went into building the prison's church.

Slade was one of forty emaciated figures pulling on two heavy ropes attached to a wooden sled loaded with granite blocks.

Linc, seated atop the granite, goaded them on—

"Pull, damn you, you worthless apes. What the hell you hangin' back fer? Who's that makin' signs at them windows?"

This last as Slade glanced toward one of the sheds that housed Confederate officers.

And as Linc recognized him—

"You'll get no help from them, you rotten reb.

An' you'll get no dinner today fer lookin' fer it."

Day after exhausting day—tugging—pulling—lifting—straining. And always Linc there—goading—driving—jeering—

Sickness—

Pneumonia in the winter, heat prostration and fever in the summer, malnutrition always. And finally—smallpox.

One after another, they were carried from the shed to the hospital. And from the hospital to the dead house, the vacated hospital bed filled by another victim while still warm from the body of his predecessor.

Slade had never liked the man who had the bunk above him; a dour, cadaverous individual with dirty personal habits—he gave off an odor like a blend of sour milk and cat urine. They had almost come to blows during one prolonged rainy spell when Slade objected to having his blanket constantly soiled by the other's muddy boots as he climbed to his bunk. But when he lay half-conscious, moaning and burning with fever, and the pustules appeared, Slade helped lift him from the bunk and carry him to the hospital.

It didn't occur to Slade until that night that he had exposed himself to the dread disease. And when he did think of it, he didn't much care. Death would be almost a relief. An escape from this torment, this exhaustion, this hopelessness without end.

And then in April there was an end. Word came of Appomatox, and a few days later, of Johnston's surrender to Sherman.

The will to live was reborn—and with it apprehension that he might be stricken before arrangements for the release of prisoners were completed. Weeks that seemed like months passed before, finally, he walked through the gate. Looked back to see a scowling Linc Weaver watch him go toward the barge-ferry that would take him to freedom.

Heat again. Dry heat now. Parching desert heat.

Then blessed moistness on his lips. Cool liquid trickling down his throat. A cool, damp cloth laving his brow, his face—his entire body.

And the face—first seen vaguely through shimmering fever haze. The face first taken for that of his sister Nedra as she cared for him after he had at last made his way back to Shelbourne Farm, emaciated and sick.

But in the cool of night, after another drink, it wasn't the face of Nedra Shelbourne, with her blue eyes and auburn hair.

This face, in the soft light of a homemade tallow candle, had black hair and dark brown eyes. One eye, the right, had a small mote, like a fleck of the pupil misplaced in the brown iris.

A wide oval face, features softly rounded. Nose slightly turned up, lips slightly full, teeth small and very white. Skin smooth-satiny with a slightly brownish tinge, reminding Slade of the hot milk lightly laced with coffee his mother permitted him as a boy on cold wintry mornings. The black hair, glinting in the candlelight, was pulled back into braids tied with pink ribbons.

She wore a simple dress of light blue, loose at the neck, revealing the slope of soft-fleshed golden tan shoulders and the rise of full rounded breasts.

"Who are you?" Slade asked, his voice faint and shaky. "Where am I?"

As he tried to raise himself up, she put small hands on his shoulders, pushing him back with an ease that made him realize how weak he was.

"Calmese, senor. Be still." Her voice was soft and liquid. "You are hurt. Enfermo—sick. Much fever. You lost much blood."

She held up her hand, tips of thumb and fore-finger a fraction of an inch apart. "Momentito, senor. I be right back."

She walked out of the candlelight. Slade looked around.

He lay on a low bed. Above him the ceiling was made of reeds woven together with fibers and lashed to rough-hewn poles. The walls were of 'dobe, unpainted dirt brown. On a table against one wall, neatly folded, were his trousers, shirt and gunbelt.

He realized that under the nubby-weave off-white bedcover he was naked except for a bandage of similar material on his left arm.

At sight of the bandage, memory flooded back. He recalled it, up to the time he had crawled from the rock into the saddle on Lady's back.

Because of his condition, and hers, Lady couldn't have carried him far. So this must be the small rancho in the arroyo.

But how long had he been here? What had become of Linc Weaver? Lady? Prince?

As the girl returned, carrying a bowl from which faint wisps of steam arose, these questions tumbled from Slade's lips. But the girl—she could be fifteen, or twenty, it was hard to tell in this country where they matured so young—held up her hand.

"Esperese, senor. Eat now, talk later."

Setting the bowl on the table, she helped him rise so that he was half sitting, back supported against the rough 'dobe. She fed him a spoonful at a time from the bowl—rice broth flavored by a few wisps of chicken.

With the soup warming his belly, those questions seemed suddenly less urgent. A languid weariness came over him, a weakness so overpowering he couldn't hold up his eyelids.

The last thing he remembered was the girl's face close before him as she moved him again flat on the bed, her lips parted in a soft smile.

Later, the dry heat of fever gripped him again. Again the moist, cooling cloth wiped his face and body. But the fever persisted until, hours later, he woke to find his body drenched with cold sweat.

In the morning the girl replaced the sodden covers below and above him. The bed, he saw, was a grass-filled mattress on a rope-strung wood frame. She brought him a bowl of warm, gray-white gruel. Slade, able to sit up and feed himself, found the stuff virtually tasteless, with a gluey consistency, but filling.

"Now," he said when he was finished, handing her back the bowl, finding his voice stronger than the night before, "those questions. First, who are you? Como se llama?"

The girl, seated beside the bed on a small stool, smiled.

"Me llamo Socorro Gonzales," she said, and added, "a mis amigos, 'Coco'." She bobbed head and shoulders in a kind of sitting curtsy. "A sus ordenes, senor."

And before Slade could decide on his second question—

"Y usted, senor—como se llama?"

Slade told her his name, then went on with his questioning. It was a slow and uncertain procedure, complicated by the language barrier. Slade's minimal Spanish sufficed for basic purposes—seeking food, drink, directions—but was inadequate for detailed conversation. The girl, though she had evidently once known English fairly well—"Until five years we live in San Diego" —had used it little since moving to Baja and spoke hesitantly.

Eventually, however, Slade learned the things he needed to know.

He was, as he had thought, at the small rancho he had looked down on from the rim of the arroyo.

But he was surprised to learn he had arrived there, semi-conscious and feverish, "anteayer"— the day before yesterday. He had been alternately delirious or in coma for more than 36 hours before regaining his senses the night before.

Coco, who had cared for him all that time, lived at the rancho with "Tio Luis"—her uncle—and her younger brother, Eduardo, whom she called Lalo. It had been Lalo, wearing a skirt of his sister's, who had brought the food up to Linc and his men while they had Slade under seige. But how, Slade wondered, did that "abajo los yanquis"—down with the yankees—square with his aiding Linc?

That, considering the language problem was too complicated a question, so Slade asked a simpler one.

"Que pasa con mi caballa?" There was a more precise word for mare, but he couldn't remember it, so he simply applied the feminine "a" to the word for horse.

Coco assured him that Lady was safe in the cactus corral. But when he asked about Prince—

"Mi otro caballo—grande—colorado—"

Light creases appeared on Coco's forehead.

"The big red horse—he is yours?"

"He sure is." In mixed English-Spanish, Slade told how Prince had been stolen from Rancho Los Robles.

The girl's dark, almost straight eyebrows drew together.

"But el gringo grande—Leenk—tell us he buy horse from you—you try to steal him back."

"Why that bastard!"

Then quickly, though the girl showed no sign of understanding the word, Slade apologized.

"Perdoname, senorita. But my horse—is he here?"

Coco shook her head.

"What about Linc?"

Her reply sounded to Slade like "Safe way." But as she added, "he go," he realized it had been the Spanish "se fue."

Linc, she continued, with Prince and the one remaining Mexican—the man Slade had shot during the sunset attack had died soon after reaching the rancho—had returned to the rancho during the night. Coco had bandaged a shallow furrow in Linc's right forearm; he and his companion had ridden out at dawn.

"Which way did they go?" Slade asked. "I've got to go after them." He struggled to get up, but waves of weakness washed over him, the room blurred as he sank back on the bed.

The girl quickly rose, dipped a cloth in a pan of water and placed it on his forehead. The room—and the girl—came back into focus. She was shaking her head at him.

"No, senor. You have been muy enfermo. You must rest. It will be muchos dias before you can go."

Actually, it was three days. In the meantime, Slade learned several things—first, that Coco's brother had accompanied Linc Weaver.

"I no want him to go," the girl said. "But el gringo grande promise mucho dinero for Lalo to go as guide."

"Guide to where?"

"No comprendo exactamente. South and east—in the mountains. To hunt for tesoro—treasure. He had a map, he showed it to Tio Luis. He wanted Tio Luis to be guide, but he would not go, so Lalo went."

That evening Slade learned more about the treasure Linc Weaver sought from Tio Luis.

A morning nap, a hearty midday meal—chicken

with rice, tamales, frijoles and tortillas—followed by a long afternoon siesta, had given Slade strength enough to dress and make his way—leaning lightly on Coco's soft but surprisingly strong shoulders—out to a chair placed under the ramada in front of the ranchhouse.

The sun had already dropped below the coastal hills when the old man came in from weeding the beanfield—because of the daytime heat all such work had to be done in the early morning or late afternoon.

With the pink-to-purple afterglow fading in the west, Tio Luis related the legend—laboriously translated by Coco, the old man knowing little English—of El Tesoro de los Indios—the Treasure of the Indians.

More than three hundred years ago, the Spanish fanned out northward after their conquest of Montezuma, hearing many stories of fabulous hoards of Indian gold—greater even than the treasure they had already stripped from the Aztecs. The stories led Coronado to search for the famed "seven cities of Cibola" and another fabled city called Quivira. Coronado, on his epic trek, found only pueblos of the Zunis and the headquarters village of the Wichitas, but the stories persisted and hordes of treasure hunters followed Coronado's example, if not his wandering footsteps.

Not a few of these did find gold—but not the Indian treasure. They found it—and even more silver—in the mountains, and they got it out with Indian slave labor at a horrible cost in Indian lives, from such places as Guanajuato, and Zacatecas, and Taxco.

"But those places are on the mainland," said Slade. "What does all this have to do with Linc Weaver and Baja California?"

As Coco translated, the old man's leather-tan, prune-crinkled face creased in a patient smile as he responded.

"Tio Luis does not truly believe the legend," Coco said. "He only repeats it."

"I'm sorry," said Slade, realizing he had been gently reprimanded. "Please ask him to go on—"

It was true, the old man continued, there had been no major gold or silver discoveries in Baja California—only a few small mines far to the south, beyond La Paz. But according to the legend, there had been mines in Baja, worked by the Indians before the coming of the Spaniards. However, seeing what was happening on the mainland, and alarmed by arrival of the first Jesuit missionaries on the peninsula, the Indians had sealed up the Baja mines so they would not be found, and they could not be forced to work them.

"Se dice tambien—it is said also," Coco translated, "that the Indians put all their gold vessels, their ornaments, in the mines before they were closed."

Ever since, there had been rumors of men finding one of the old Indian mines. But if anyone ever actually found any gold, they had better sense than to talk about it and give the government tax collectors an excuse to take it away from them.

There were also men who claimed they had found such mines, but were unable for one reason or another to explore them fully. Many of these men made maps of the supposed location of the mines, and if the mapmaker, because of age, infirmity, or lack of time or money, could not return to the mine, he might be persuaded—for a suitable sum—to sell his map.

In time, there came to be a good many of these maps in circulation. Tio Luis, in his lifetime, had seen several, but had never heard of anyone finding the mine they purported to show. Still, there was the problem of the tax collector. Perhaps—

Linc Weaver's map looked old—it could be authentic. The area it showed, in the massive mountain range called San Pedro Martir, was familiar to Tio Luis.

But the old man, although he was offered forty dollars in gold to serve as guide, begged off on grounds that the trip would be too strenuous for someone of his sixty-some years.

But when Linc got Lalo aside and showed him the map—promised him half as much money as he'd offered Tio Luis—the boy, his 16-year-old imagination fired by visions of treasure, agreed to go. He was familiar with the area, having visited it on hunting trips with Tio Luis, and was sure he could find the landmarks noted on the map.

"I no want him to go," Coco said. "It is very wild country—primitivo. There are hombres malos —even indios—muy salvaje—savage. And I no trust el gringo grande before—now I know he steal your horse—"

Her worried brown eyes looked at Slade, shifted to Tio Luis, back to Slade.

"I'm going after them," said Slade. "Just as soon—"

He started to rise, but his legs gave way and he sank back into the chair.

Coco and Tio Luis helped him back to the bed, where he soon fell into an exhausted sleep filled with more nightmarish visions of Fort Delaware, followed by a graphic dream of his return to Shelbourne Farm.

Everything looked the same as Slade trudged wearily up the long lane from the Danville Pike. The simple but imposing two-story white house with its broad veranda across the front and south side. The big elm shading the southwest corner of the house, which stood on a slight rise. The colorful shrubs surrounding it—alternating pink and white oleander, bright yellow acacia. Green lawns lush from late-spring rains.

But the lawns, he saw as he drew nearer, were weed-choked and long unmowed. The shrubs were unpruned and tangled, and straggly tendrils of honeysuckle overhung the veranda. Big strips of paint had peeled from the facings and broad-beamed pillars of the veranda, even the house siding, revealing weather-grayed wood beneath.

When he tugged at the bell-pull it came away in his hand without so much as a tinkle. He pounded on the door until it finally opened and a wizened black face topped by kinky white hair peered out.

"Why, it be Master Slade," a voice crackled—a voice he barely recognized as that of Old Henry, his father's head house nigger. Old Henry hadn't really been that old; the name distinguished him from his son, Young Henry, the head groom. But he certainly deserved it now. He seemed to have aged a decade for each year of the war.

But if Old Henry was aged, Slade's grandfather was ancient, he found after the black man had shufflingly led him into the gloomy parlor.

Sherman Shelbourne sat in the wheelchair he'd been confined to since suffering a stroke when told his only son had been killed at Shiloh. The chair faced the French doors onto the south veranda, where partly-drawn maroon velvet drapes admitted the only daylight to the room.

A velveteen smoking jacket, greenish with age, hung loosely over thin, stooped shoulders. Moving to his side, Slade saw that the once proudly patrician head was now little more than a fleshless skull overlayed by thin wisps of straight white hair. Once piercing blue eyes were now washed-out gray, deeply sunk in shadowy sockets. There was no recognition in those eyes as Slade stepped in front of him.

"Grandfather—"

The old man remained quiet, but another voice spoke from the doorway—

"Slade? Oh, Slade!"

Quick light footsteps crossed the worn carpet, his sister Nedra threw herself into his arms.

"Oh, Slade, Slade, you're back—you've come home! Oh I'm so happy to see you—but Slade honey, you're so thin—what have they done to you?"

He told her, briefly, sparing the worst details. As

he talked, he studied his sister. The pretty but rather pudgy, round-cheeked girl of 17 he had left when he rode off to join Morgan had been transformed by years of wartime hardships into a slender young woman of aristocratic beauty. Soft-falling reddish-brown hair framed a finely modeled face whose flawless complexion was lightly flushed with excitement. Slade was strongly reminded of his mother, dead these ten years.

". . .and that's about it," Slade concluded. "Here I am. And how about you. You're certainly looking well."

"Oh, I'm all right," his sister said, "considering—"

A shrug of straight shoulders and a tossing head gesture indicated the house—all of Shelbourne Farm.

Slade nodded toward the old man in the wheelchair.

"And grandfather?"

Nedra's eyes fell.

"He's been this way almost a year. Doctor McTavish says it can't be much longer. I"—her voice broke—"I hope he's right. It's awful—he just sits there all day, every day, looking out."

Looking, Slade realized, at the gently rolling fenced paddocks off beyond the stud barn.

Looking at them, but was he seeing them? And if he was seeing them, was he seeing them as they used to be, with a score or more of broodmares, stiff-legged foals at their sides at this time of year; beyond them in the big pasture a gang of yearlings racing around, playing, confronting each other with mock ferocity? Or was he seeing them as they were today—virtually empty?

Before the war, the Thoroughbred population of Shelbourne Farm ranged from sixty to ninety, depending on whether crop of three-year-olds had been taken east to the sales.

Now, Slade learned, it was down to four—two aged broodmares, barren the past two seasons because there was no stallion fit to breed them to, plus Warrior Prince and Shelbourne Lady. And Prince and Lady had been saved from Union horse-hunters only because Young Henry kept them hidden in a shack behind an old share-cropper's cabin, deep in Shelbourne Wood.

The farm was little better off in other respects. Throughout the war supplies had been commandeered not only for Union troops stationed in Kentucky, but for those fighting to the south and the east. By war's end the only livestock left at Shelbourne, besides the horses, one very old English setter and several cats, was a double handful of hens and one rooster. All the grains were gone, even the seed grain, so there was nothing with which to plant crops. If it weren't for a scattering of fruit trees, a truck garden Young Henry somehow kept going, and the lush Kentucky bluegrass for the horses—

"We'd all have starved," Nedra said matter-of-factly.

As it was, she'd been getting by on credit, backed by the prestige of the Shelbourne name and the hypothetical value of the Shelbourne land. Credit first from local merchants, later from the bank, to pay off the merchants.

"Two thousand, eight hundred dollars," Nedra said, pointing one long, slender finger at the latest entry in the account book. "That's what we owe Commercial Mercantile. I have eighteen dollars and twenty cents in the house. And Brent Marshall says he can't possibly let us have another cent."

"Brent Marshall?" said Slade. "Is he running the bank now?"

Nedra nodded. "Since he got home six weeks ago. His father's awfully sick—his lungs—he was just holding on until Brent got back."

"I'll go see him tomorrow," said Slade.

But that night, fever gripped him—the reaction from his long imprisonment and the exhausting journey home. It was two weeks before he was able to saddle Prince and ride into town.

Brent Marshall, established in his father's musty office in the Commercial Mercantile Bank of Lexington, didn't want to talk about money. He wanted to talk about war experiences—his with Stuart, Slade's with Morgan.

"Brent," Slade said finally at the conclusion of the other's account of Stuart's final fight at Yellow Tavern, "I've got to have money—and time—to get Shelbourne Farm back on its feet."

"I wish I could," said the banker—who was only a few years older than Slade. "But the way things are now—"

"Say twelve hundred dollars," Slade went on. "Make it an even four thousand we owe. I'll sign a mortgage—principal and interest due in five years."

"Can't give you that long," said Marshall. "Two years at the most."

Slade signed the papers and struggled—with young Henry—sometimes even Nedra helping out with lighter chores in the fields—but it didn't work.

In December of '66, a month after Sherman Shelbourne finally died in his sleep, Slade went again to Brent Marshall's office.

"I can't make it, Brent," he said frankly. "I'll need more money—and more time."

The banker shook his head.

"Just a few hundred dollars—until next spring. Prince is ready to race—there'll be some meetings—"

Again Brent Marshall shook his head.

"There'll be no race meetings for at least another year. Not enough horses—not enough money. I'm sorry, Slade."

"Then you'll have to take Shelbourne Farm," Slade said, trying to keep anger out of his voice, rising to his feet.

"I don't want to do that." Brent Marshall stared at his cluttered desk. "I'm no farmer. I'm not sure I'm a banker, but I'm sure as hell no farmer."

He looked up.

"Tell you what—if you plant tobacco, I can advance you more against the crop, extend the mortgage."

Plant tobacco at Shelbourne Farm? Plow up those bluegrass paddocks and pastures for tobacco?

Slowly, Slade shook his head.

He didn't sleep at all that night. Turned and tossed, trying to figure out some way—

If only there would be racing in Kentucky next spring. He could win enough money with Prince to pay off the loan, maybe race Lady too, for awhile, then breed her—why in no time Shelbourne Farm would be on its feet again.

Maybe Brent Marshall was wrong.

But Slade knew he was right. Thanks to Young Henry, he had Prince and Lady—few other horse people in Kentucky had been that lucky. And even if there had been enough decent horses of racing age, with the country still suffering the economic ravages of war, little money could be made from racing.

Rolling over and punching at his pillow, Slade suddenly thought of something he'd heard Linc Weaver say in the Columbus Penitentiary. Telling about his experiences in California, about the splendid horses of the native Californios—and their love for gambling.

"They'll bet on anything," Linc had said. "and on their horses, they'll bet everything. Money—jewels—their home—their rancho—likely they'd even bet their women."

Slade was in Brent Marshall's office early the next morning, explaining his plan.

"Six thousand more," he said. "Make it an even ten thousand. Five hundred for Nedra to keep the place going, five hundred for traveling money—five thousand for stake money. Give us until the end of next year—"

"What the hell do you take me for," said Brent,

"a banker or a gambler?"

But there was a glint in his eyes.

"A Kentucky banker," said Slade, responding to that glint.

He got the money—at five per cent above the usual interest rate.

A throbbing pain in his arm made Slade realize he was lying on his left side. He realized too that at some point—he couldn't remember exactly when—the dream had become half-waking memory.

He turned over and soon fell into a deep and dreamless sleep.

Chapter 6

Slade awoke to the first gray light seeping through a small window. Soon he heard sounds in the outside kitchen area, and a little later smelled coffee brewing.

"Buenos dias."

Coco, smiling, came into the room carrying a steaming cup of coffee and a bowl of the gray-white gruel, which she called atole.

When Slade had finished the atole and coffee, the girl removed the bandage from his arm and together they examined the wound. The inflamation seemed to have subsided considerably, though the hole where the slug had exited on the inner side of the arm was still red and puffy.

Coco left, returning in a few minutes carrying a plate on which was a small lump of what looked like minced stewed greens—and smelled like rotten fish boiled in castor oil.

"My God," cried Slade, "do you expect me to eat that?"

The girl giggled.

"No senor—is for your arm—to draw out poison."

Squeezing moisture out of the lump of what on closer inspection proved to be a mixture of leathery leaves, pulped twigs and roots, she applied it to the inner arm wound and rewrapped the bandage. Then she helped Slade on with his shirt and fashioned a sling from a large square of the coarse gray white cloth.

The girl left and Slade got out of bed, finding he could stand alone, though his legs still felt wobbly. He pulled on trousers and boots, looked around for his hat and remembered he'd left it on the big rock up on the rim of the arroyo, along with his carbine.

His first impulse was to hurry up there and get the gun. Then he realized this was both impractical, in his condition, and unnecessary. The odds against anyone finding the gun, in such a sparsely populated country, were astronomical. And the carbine sure as hell wouldn't rust in this arid climate.

Nevertheless, after a day of doing nothing more strenuous than sitting around watching Coco perform her household duties, when Tio Luis came in from the fields about an hour before sundown, Slade asked him to saddle Lady. Hauling himself laboriously onto the mare's back, he headed up the trail.

As expected, he found the carbine, the boxes of cartridges, and his sombrero undisturbed.

Riding back down the trail into the arroyo, Slade looked beyond the far rim to the distant bulk of the San Pedro Martir range.

Linc Weaver, having lost two men and been nicked himself, had evidently decided to abandon his attempt to kill Slade and go hunt for the lost mine—taking Prince with him.

Which meant Slade had to follow. Did Linc anticipate this? Would he set up an ambush somewhere along the trail? Slade recalled his earlier apprehension along those lines, when he first set out from Rancho Los Robles.

There was only one way to find out. Push on south.

"Manana," he told Coco and Tio Luis a little later, as they were eating the evening meal by candlelight in the larger of the ranchhouse's two rooms. "Manana yo voy"—his Spanish broke down—"after them. After el gringo. Can your uncle make a map so I can find the place where the mine is supposed to be?"

After a brief exchange with Tio Luis, Coco replied—

"He could make a map, senor, but it would be muy dificil—difficult—for you to follow. Better he go and show you."

"But I thought," said Slade, "the trip was too—dificil—for him at his age."

"He only say this because he no trust el gringo grande. He can go."

"I'll pay him," Slade said. But Coco shook her head.

"Is no need, senor. He wants to go. We both tenemos miedo—we are afraid—for Lalo. So he will go with you, to guide you."

They could not, however, leave the next morning as Slade wanted. Tio Luis considered it unsafe to leave Coco alone at the rancho.

"Bad men back in the hills," the girl explained, "and Indians—sometimes they attack the ranchos."

Slade had heard of the roving bands of desperadoes—white, brown and black—that plagued the border area. Law and order, none too effective even after almost twenty years of American rule north of the line, was virtually non-existent south of it. Especially now, with Mexico only recently free from foreign rule. Scarcely two months ago, Napoleon's puppet, Maximilian, had been executed at Queretaro.

As for Indians, though their numbers had been decimated by the changed life style and disease—especially smallpox and syphilis, brought by the Spanish—small, primitive bands still held out in Baja California and across the Sea of Cortez in Sonora. In San Diego, they still spoke with horror of people slaughtered and two girls carried off into captivity in a raid some years earlier on Rancho Jamul. There had been raids on other ranchos—and missions—since.

The next morning Tio Luis saddled his mule—Lalo, accompanying Linc Weaver, had ridden the mount of one of the dead horsethieves—and headed up the arroyo. There was another rancho about ten miles away, operated by a large family. In midafternoon the old man returned with a kindly-looking man of about sixty, his rotund wife and one of their sons, a man of about thirty.

The newcomers had brought a half-grown goat. It was promptly killed and dressed. Coco and the older woman busied themselves in the kitchen area while the men sat out front under the ramada, talking.

"We no see them long time," Coco explained to Slade as she passed around a platter of toasted tortilla sections topped with beans and melted cheese. "Tonight we have small fiesta."

The small fiesta featured barbecued kid, roasted corn, beans with cheese and tortillas hot from an iron griddle, washed down with wine and later a bottle of brandy. The wine was red and more than slightly sour, the brandy sweet and tasting of raisins. They came, Coco told Slade, from a rancho to the north, established on the site of one of the old missions, Santo Tomas. He suspected it was the large rancho he had avoided on the way down.

They talked long into the night, sitting in front of the house. At first a single candle cast its glow on their faces—the lined, worn faces of Tio Luis and the old man, like images carved in lustrous mahogany; the lean, dark features of the younger man, contrasting with Coco's softly rounded, creamy-tan countenance.

Their Spanish was generally too rapid, the accents too slurred, for Slade to understand much of what they said. But from words he did catch, and explanatory comments from Coco, seated beside him, they spoke mostly about their neighbors —in this country anyone living within a hundred miles north or south was a neighbor. About births, deaths, illnesses, injuries, marriages.

They talked too about the weather—especially rain. Rain governed the crops, and in this non-monetary economy, crops meant life. Wet years and dry years came in cycles, Coco said. In the rainy cycles there was plenty for all, and even some surplus to be hauled north to sell, at other ranchos or even as far as San Diego. But in dry cycles the animals were killed for their meat; then the people took the road north to look for work. Only the Indians remained, living on natural grains, roots, some types of cactus, small animals, snakes, insects—

The past few years, Coco said, there had been ample winter rains. Recalling the parched country he'd ridden through, Slade wondered what it could possibly be like in a dry cycle.

The moon was high overhead and the brandy bottle empty when Tio Luis stretched, yawned, and said "Tengo sueno—vamos a dormir."

In the first pale gray of pre-dawn, Slade awoke to the gentle touch of Coco's hand on his shoulder.

"Come senor—you must get early start."

In the other room, while Slade was sipping coffee by candlelight, the girl examined his arm. The inflamation had subsided considerably.

"I think is all right," Coco said as she wound a fresh strip of cloth around his bicep. "But you wear this for two-three days," she added, replacing the sling.

Outside, Tio Luis waited with Lady and the mule. The old man attached wide wings of stiff-tanned leather to their saddle bows to protect their legs against brush and cactus—"armas," he called them.

Before mounting, Slade turned to the girl, reached out and took her hand.

"Thank you—muchas gracias—Coco—for everything."

Her small, soft hand squeezed his.

"Para servirle, senor."

"Look," he said, "my name isn't 'senor.' It's Slade."

He gazed for a moment into her eyes, then quickly turned away and rather clumsily, because he had to grab the horn with his right hand, swung up into the saddle.

Coco smiled up at him.

"Vaya con dios," she said, "senor Slade."

The moon, waning now toward its last quarter, was still showing above the coastal hills as they rode up the south side of the arroyo. When they reached the top, Slade swung around in the saddle and looked back.

A small figure stood beside the ranchhouse. Slade held up his right arm. Coco waved.

When he looked again a few minutes later the ranchhouse was out of sight below the rim of the arroyo. Only the lazily turning arms of the windmill were visible. The slowly spinning vanes struck Slade as symbolic of the way of life in this scorching, sun-baked land. A slow, simple way of life—and entirely dependent upon the whims of nature.

As the sun came up, Slade found himself listening to the silence of the wilderness through which they moved. The only sounds were the clump-clop of hoofs on sandy soil, the creaking of saddle leather, rarely the chirp of a bird, the buzz of a rattlesnake.

Slade had enjoyed the pre-war tranquillity of rural Kentucky. But at Shelbourne Farm there was continuous activity—slaves taking care of the horses and the fields—trips to town for supplies—

the Sunday excursion to church—visiting back and forth with neighbors.

Here in Baja California the distances were so vast, the inhabitants so few, it seemed almost as though Slade and the old man were the only two human beings in the universe.

That they weren't was demonstrated by the octagonal-barreled old muzzle-loader Tio Luis carried across the saddle bow, and the way he continually turned his head to examine the surrounding country.

At midmorning, with the full force of the sun blazing down, the old man turned off the trail into a narrow, steep-banked arroyo overhung by brush —sparse but capable of giving some shade. Tio Luis dismounted.

"Quedamos aqui," he said, "algunas horas."

Slade made that to mean wait here several hours, and he didn't like it.

He tried to convey his urgency to Tio Luis, saying it was "muy importante" to go "rapido—rapido." But the old man replied, using a combination of Spanish and sign language, that it was "muy importante" to go "despacio—no rapido" because "el sol"—pointing to the sun— was "muy caliente—muy malo para los caballos" —indicating Lady and the mule.

He unsaddled and picketed their mounts, spread a blanket close up against the shady side of the arroyo and lay down with head pillowed on arm and wide-brimmed straw sombrero over his head. Soon gentle snoring sounds came from under the hat.

Slade scrunched himself up against a bank of the arroyo and sat; sweating, fuming and fidgeting.

He could understand the need for a midday break. He had taken them himself, to rest Lady, while trailing the horsethieves from Los Robles. But to halt at midmorning, for several hours—

He couldn't waste that much time. Counting back, he figured it was nine days since Prince had been stolen. Tio Luis had said it would take four days to get to the area of the lost mine. And even if they found Linc Weaver and regained Prince immediately, it would take a week or more to get back to San Diego. Which would be well into September, and the race was scheduled September 15.

Time was all-important—yet the old man lay there sleeping.

When the sun had crossed the arroyo so Tio Luis was exposed to its heat, he stirred, sat up and rubbed his eyes, moved to a shady spot under the other bank and went back to sleep.

It was at least another two hours before the old man again awakened. He watered the horses— borrowing Slade's hat. In addition to Slade's canteens, Tio Luis had brought a large goatskin bag of water. From another bag he took some meat and some bread—they ate. Finally, with the sun only a couple of hours above the horizon, they returned to the trail.

When it was almost full dark they made a dry camp and munched more meat and cakes of dried corn meal, washed down with water. When the old man rolled up in his blanket, Slade did likewise.

But it seemed he had barely dozed off when Tio Luis was shaking him awake.

"Levantese, senor—vamos a viajar por la luna."

As the moon rose above the eastern hills, they continued south.

Except for occasional pauses to rest their mounts and stretch their own legs, they rode on throughout the night and until the sun was high and hot in mid-morning.

They camped in a canyon under a solitary old oak. After another unappetizing but sustaining meal, as Slade dropped wearily down on his blanket, he realized how the horsethieves, riding south from Los Robles, had outdistanced him half a day in three days. By traveling at night and laying up during the heat of the day they were able to cover far more miles with less fatigue for both men and animals.

Late that afternoon the trail dipped into a steep-sided arroyo, formed by water slicing through a low hill. At one point the south side consisted of an almost-sheer wall of rock over a hundred feet high. At its base, in a level slab of volcanic rock, were several pools of water similar to those Slade had found the night before reaching Tio Luis's rancho.

"Tinajas," the old man said. "Tienen agua todo el ano"—which Slade took to mean there was water—such as it was, scummy and stagnant—here all year round.

Nearby, the old man pointed out the ashy remains of a fire.

"Los otros," he said, "algunos dias pasado."

Slade grunted. He didn't need to be reminded

Linc was several days ahead of them. If only there was some way—

A thought occurred to him. Carefully he phrased a question in Spanish.

"Hay una ruta mas derecho—mas rapido?"

Tio Luis nodded.

"Si—hay. Pero es muy dificil, y peligroso. Es posible encontraremos indios—"

"Hell with Indians," said Slade. "I want to get my horse back—pronto!"

And groping again for Spanish words—

"Cuanto tiempo menos—esta ruta?"

"Creo un dia, mas o menos."

A day more or less. Was it worth it? What if Linc had already found the mine, loaded up with gold, was on his way back? They might miss him.

What, Slade asked himself, would John Hunt Morgan do?

"Vamos por esta ruta corta," he told Tio Luis.

When the moon finally appeared—as it waned it rose later and later—they saddled up. Feeling his arm was sufficiently healed, Slade discarded his sling and helped with this task.

They rode slowly, Tio Luis scanning the ground carefully. After about an hour he halted, pointed to the east.

"Vamos arriba—a la sierra," he said, leading the way toward distant mountains.

They rode through slowly rising hills, following a trail now faint and overgrown. At one time it must have been heavily traveled; in places its surface was noticeably depressed from the surrounding ground.

"Un camino viejo?" Slade asked.

"Muy viejo. Un camino de los padres—y antes, de los indios."

As the old missionary-Indian trail climbed higher, chaparral became thicker and larger. Trees became numerous—scrub oak and stiff-branched, red-barked manzanita. Packed between the trees was sage and other brush, much of it with long, sharp thorns. Slade was thankful for the heavy leather armas protecting his legs from stiff, tearing branches. Sometimes Tio Luis had to dismount to hack a path through dense growth with a machete.

Soon after sunrise the terrain became more broken. The trail entered an arroyo leading up into the hills. As they climbed, the arroyo became narrower, more choked with brush.

Then, rounding a bend, Slade saw a wall of rock far ahead—a sheer escarpment several hundred feet high, stretching as far as the eye could see to either side.

The sun was broiling down from above when they paused to water their mounts in an oak-studded clearing. After a brief rest, they pushed on.

As they neared the escarpment, Slade saw that its face, which had looked smooth from a distance, had been cut into deep grooves by water and wind erosion.

The trail led into the base of one of these grooves through a passage so narrow Slade could almost have touched the wall on each side. After a few yards the trail angled to the right and climbed steeply.

Following Tio Luis's example, Slade swung down from the saddle. Carefully they led their mounts up the defile, in places so choked with piled boulders as to be almost impassable. Their progress was punctuated by the clatter of dislodged stones and the scrape of hoofs slipping and sliding on the rocky surface.

Once a big rock turned under Lady's hoof and she went almost to her knees. Slade's heart skipped several beats, but the mare recovered and continued with no sign of injury.

Though the precipitous sides of the defile shaded them from the sun, long before they reached the top, Slade's shirt was soaked dark with sweat.

Emerging finally from the chasm, Slade looked out over the rim of the escarpment and saw, beyond rolling miles of brush-covered hills, the sea, burnished by the late-afternoon sun.

Continuing east, they found the going, though still uphill, easier. There was less chaparral and more trees—small fork-topped pines, junipers, several varieties of oak.

As the sun neared the sea behind them, ahead they were confronted by another escarpment. Though this wall at first looked as formidable as the other, when they got close Slade saw that it was broken by a broad arroyo, which they rode up with relative ease. They came out on a broad, slightly rolling tableland that stretched apparently unbroken for many miles to north and south.

Now there were grasses and low shrubs underfoot. Tio Luis turned south on a trail that meandered through park-like pine forest. They came to an arroyo with a shallow stream of trickling water. Lady and Tio Luis's mule dipped their muzzles and drank—Slade and the old man dismounted and did likewise.

On the other side of the stream they made camp. But though wood was plentiful, and the air turned suddenly chill in the high altitude, Tio Luis made only a small fire to heat coffee.

"Indios," he said. "Muchos Indios vienen aqui."

Waiting for the moon to rise, they slept—Slade for the first time in a long while grateful for the warmth of his blankets.

By moonlight, they continued south. Twice they traveled the length of broad, grassy meadows. Then the trail angled to the east, until, with the moon high overhead, they were confronted by a sight that took Slade's breath away.

Ahead, rock-slab sides silver in the moonlight, towered a precipitous peak.

Between them and the peak, shadowy and ghost-like, was a deep-cleft canyon slanting down, then bending east until it funneled out onto a broad, barren desert plain. Beyond the plain, glistening in the pale silver light, was a broad expanse of water —what Slade knew must be the Sea of Cortez.

Tio Luis pointed to the peak.

"Picacho del Diablo. Alla, dice la mapa del gringo grande, es La Mina de Los Indios."

Slade stared at the moon-silvered peak.

So this was where Linc Weaver would look for the lost mine.

He wondered—was Linc already here?

As though in answer, a sound broke the stillness, hitherto disturbed only by the gentle sighing of the wind in the pines at their backs.

A sharp sound, its source unmistakable.

The blast of a gun, amplified by a thousand echoes as it floated up to them from the depths of the canyon.

Chapter 7

Slade's first thought on hearing the shot was that they'd ridden into the ambush he feared. But no slug buzzed by his head, and he quickly realized the sound had echoed up from the depths of the canyon, far out of range.

His second thought was to investigate.

"Let's get down there," he said. "Vamos abajo."

But the old man held up his hand; listened.

There was no further gunfire. No sound except the wind in the pines, the soft breathing of Lady and the mule.

"Vamanos!" Slade said.

Tio Luis shook his head.

"Muy peligroso ahora. En la manana, cuando hay luz—"

Looking into the shadowy depths, Slade could well believe the canyon was too dangerous to negotiate by moonlight, that they'd have to wait 'til dawn.

He followed the old man back through the pine forest until they came to a small meadow, at its lower end a seepage pool. After watering and picketing Lady and the mule, they rolled up in their blankets and slept.

They were up when the first tinge of gray filtered through the pinetops bordering the meadow. But as Slade picked up his saddle, Tio Luis said, "No senor—no podemos usar los caballos."

Afoot, each carrying a full canteen, they followed a shallow arroyo to the rim of the canyon, and in the growing light Slade saw why they couldn't use the horses.

The canyon between them and the peak was a monstrous carving of nature, filled with huge, slab-sided boulders piled on top of each other, vertical cliff faces and rock chimneys, sculptured over eons by water and gale-blown sand.

There was an escarpment on this side of the mountaintop plateau, too. Though not as high as those to the west, it dropped away sharply, sheer cliffs broken only by steep runoff arroyos and an occasional talus slide of fragmented rock.

The arroyo they were following became almost vertical, a rounded tube cut out of granite by cataract carryoff of torrential mountain rains. Descent was possible only because swirling water action had formed ridges providing hand and footholds. Still Slade felt as though he were crawling down the cutaway half of a gigantic bottleneck.

After a hundred feet the angle of descent eased. The bottleneck became a V-shaped gorge angling toward the main canyon.

With Tio Luis in the lead, surprisingly agile in spite of his gimp leg, they worked their way down the brush and rock-choked gorge into the main canyon and went up it slowly, often hopping from boulder to boulder across patches of low brush and cactus. From time to time they heard the crisp, dry buzz of a nearby rattler.

Finally, where a steep side canyon came in from the east, they came to a broad, rock-cluttered clearing, at the far end of which was a large pool of fresh water. A few yards from the pool they found a rock-rimmed fire ring, and not far away the remains of a bighorn ewe.

This, Slade figured, was the source of the shot they'd heard last night. Linc had staked out the waterhole and killed the sheep for fresh meat. The carcass had been partly butchered—tongue, liver and a hindquarter were gone.

Though the carcass was abuzz with flies and black with ants, Slade was tempted to cut off some of the other quarter and cook it. But smoke from a fire would betray their presence. Anyway, there wasn't time. Maybe on the way back—if there was anything left—

After resting a few minutes and drinking from the pool, they started up the side canyon toward the slab-granite upper slopes of the mountain.

They continued boulder-hopping, climbing and scrambling upward, sometimes over shifting talus slides at the base of cliffs. Once they came to a dead-end, a sheer cliff fifty feet high sealing off the canyon. Tio Luis shook his head, muttered to himself, and backtracked until he found a trail that took them up and around the barrier.

To this point they had been shaded from the sun, first by the east side of the main canyon, then by the bulk of the mountain. But now the sun appeared over the shoulder of the mountain, blazed down into their faces.

Within minutes Slade's shirt was dripping wet, clinging to his body. At the same time he became aware that his boots, far from comfortable for walking, were no footgear for mountain climbing. He could feel his feet swelling inside the leather, his toes chafing where the ends of the boots narrowed.

And he wondered—why the hell are we climbing this mountain, anyway?

To find Linc, who was looking for a gold mine.

But Slade wasn't looking for a mine. He was looking for Prince.

And as he and Tio Luis had left their mounts up on the high plateau, Linc and his party must have done the same.

So why not go back up on the plateau, hunt for Prince up there?

Two reasons.

First, the search might take a long time.

Second, Tio Luis hadn't come down here only to get Slade's horse back. The old man was worried about his nephew.

A flurry of motion ahead interrupted Slade's thoughts.

The snake hadn't rattled.

As the old man reached up for a handhold on the rock on which it was basking, warming its blood from the nighttime chill, it simply struck.

"Caray!" the old man bit out as he drew back his hand.

Slade stepped forward, drew the Colt. But Tio Luis caught his arm.

"No," he said, nodding toward the mountain. "Los otros—"

Then it was too late—the snake slithered into the brush.

"Did he bite you?" Slade asked. Though he spoke in English, the old man understood. He held up his left hand and Slade saw the fang punctures on the index finger, just above the knuckle.

What followed happened too fast for Slade to interfere.

Tio Luis, gun slung over his shoulder by a short length of rope tied to barrel and stock, had been carrying his machete in his right hand, using it occasionally to slash away brush.

Now in one swift motion he raised the machete, placed his left hand, forefinger extended, on the edge of the same rock on which the snake had been lying, and with one blow hacked off the finger just behind the knuckle.

Blood spurted out over the gray surface of the rock.

Tio Luis dropped the machete, with his good hand tried to undo the knot at the back of the kerchief around his neck.

Slade quickly loosed his own bandana and wrapped it tightly around the finger-stump. The old man raised his arm above his head and rested it against the rock.

"Gracias, senor," he said calmly, though sweat poured down his face and the skin around his lips had turned from nut brown to ash gray.

Blood soaking through the bandana-bandage trickled down his hand and wrist to disappear into the sleeve of his shirt.

"Un cigarro, senor, por favor?"

Slade rolled a cigarette, placed it between the old man's lips and lit it. He then made one for himself.

By the time they had smoked the cigarettes, the blood was no longer running down the old man's wrist. He reached up and unwound the bandana, handed it to Slade, and examined the stump of his finger, from which blood still oozed.

"Tabaco, por favor," he said. Slade poured the tobacco remaining in his pouch into Tio Luis's cupped right hand. He packed it around the stump. By gestures he indicated that Slade should cut a strip from the bandana. When he had wrapped this around the wound, he said matter of factly—

"Bueno—vamos arriba."

And as though nothing had happened, he led the way up the canyon.

Another hour and the canyon opened onto a sloping shoulder that skirted the base of a nearly perpendicular cliff. As they worked their way along the shoulder a trail became visible, wending its way through brush and huge boulders.

They paused to rest in the slender sliver of shade provided by one of these rocks, and drink a little water from their canteens. Before they started out again, Tio Luis laid his uninjured forefinger to his lips—

"Estamos cerca," he whispered. "No hable mas."

Stepping carefully, they continued a short way, until the old man halted abruptly. Easing up behind him, Slade peered past his frayed straw sombrero.

The trail continued another twenty yards or so

through a scattering of smaller rocks to a bench of bare, level ground about ten yards wide, bordered on one side by the high cliff; on the other by brush-covered slopes.

Near the far end of the flat space—another twenty yards—the cliffline was broken by a slanting jumble of stones and slabs of rock. A little beyond, the bench melded into the steep cliffs.

End of the trail.

Linc Weaver, rifle in the crook of his arm, stood watching his one remaining horsethief henchman and the youth, Lalo, as they cleared stones from the slide at the base of the cliff. Judging from the size of the rockpile off to one side, they'd been at it for some time. Evidently Linc believed the slide covered the entrance to the lost mine.

Slade, carbine cocked, started to step forward, but halted as Lalo called—

"Senor—mira!"

Thinking the youth had seen him, Slade froze. But Lalo wasn't looking his way. He was pointing at the cliff.

"Una cueva, senor. Hay una cueva aqui!"

Linc propped his rifle against the cliff and himself began hoisting stones and flinging them aside.

Motioning for Tio Luis to follow, Slade walked forward. As they drew closer, he saw that only Linc, a revolver sagging from his gunbelt, was now armed. The other man's gunbelt and rifle lay atop a pile of canvas sacks nearby.

When Slade and the old man were only a few yards away, Lalo looked up and saw them. He didn't speak, just stopped working and stared.

"Godamit, kid, git to work," Linc growled.

As Lalo stood still, transfixed, Linc turned and saw Slade and Tio Luis, their guns leveled.

The big man's hand hovered about four inches from the butt of his revolver.

Slade, memories of Fort Delaware filling his mind, hoped he'd draw. His finger was tense on the carbine's trigger. His eyes were zeroed in on the exact center of Linc's sweat-darkened, dirty-gray shirt. He found himself holding an indrawn breath.

He let the breath out slowly as Linc's hand moved away from the gunbutt.

"All right, Shelbourne," he grated, glaring defiantly, "You've got the drop—what you aim to do with it?"

"Las pistolas—los rifles," Slade barked at Tio Luis. The old man, careful to keep out of the line of fire, plucked the revolver from Linc's holster, collected his rifle and the rifle and gunbelt of the other man.

Slade advanced until the muzzle of the carbine was only a couple of yards from Linc's bulging belly.

"I'm going to gutshoot you, Linc, and leave you here."

And after a pause to let that sink in—

"Unless you answer one question. Where's my horse?"

Defiance still blazed from the big man's pale blue eyes, but when Slade took a menacing half step closer Linc's gaze shifted to the evergreen-studded plateau beyond the canyon.

"Left him over on the mesa."

Slade jerked the carbine in the direction of the trail.

"Let's go. If my horse is all right, maybe I won't kill you. Maybe I'll just leave you."

Linc started toward the trail, then hesitated, looked back at the rockslide.

"Wait a minute, Shelbourne. This here—"

"I know," said Slade. "It's supposed to be an old Indian mine. You have a map."

Linc nodded.

"Right. And the man I got the map from—he says it's more than a mine. He says when the padres came, the Injins toted their gold up here, cached it in the mine, slid rocks down to cover it."

Slade, about to say he didn't give a damn about mines or gold, hesitated. After all, why had he come all the way from Kentucky? To get money to pay off the mortgage on Shelbourne Farm. If there was gold here for the taking—

"All right," he said, nodding toward the rockslide, "get at it."

Linc said something in Spanish to the small, dark man, whom he called Mono, and to the boy, and the three of them resumed the task of moving stones. In a few minutes there was an opening big enough to pass through. Linc stuck his head inside, then pulled back.

"Dark as hell in thar. Need a torch."

Tio Luis had anticipated the problem and stepped forward with a bundle of dry brush. He started to hand it to Linc, but Slade reached out and took it. He wanted to see for himself it there was gold in the cave, and he wasn't going to give Linc a chance for any tricks with the torch. As further precaution he handed his carbine to Tio Luis and drew the Colt, a handier close-range weapon.

"Let's go," he said when the brush was lighted, gesturing with the revolver for Linc to enter first.

Through the narrow opening they stepped into a cavern about ten yards deep and twice as wide.

Slade made out dark spots on the inverted-bowl ceiling. As smoke from the torch spiraled upward he realized the smudges must have come from Indian cooking fires.

His gaze shifted to the rear wall of the cavern, and he sucked in his breath.

In the flickering light he could make out primitive paintings blazened across the stone in dramatic reds and blacks. Huge figures of men in feather headdresses and black pants, arms upraised as though in religious exhortation. Antlered animals—unmistakably deer—two of them faced off for a horned duel. A puma poised in mid-leap.

An exclamation from Linc jerked Slade's attention away from the paintings.

"Look! Over here! Fetch the torch—"

The big man hurried toward the far corner of the cave. Slade followed, torch in left hand, revolver in right. He came up behind Linc, looked down at a loose pile of objects. A pile almost two feet high and ten feet across.

Objects of many sorts—bowls—dishes—jars—cups—and many sizes. But all of essentially the same color—the rich, gleaming dark-yellow of nearly pure gold!

"Here it is!" Linc gasped. "Injin gold! And look—thar's where it comes from."

Slade's eyes followed Linc's pointing finger.

Beyond the pile of gold was a deep fissure in the cave wall, extending back several yards into the solid rock. Toolmarks on walls, floor and ceiling indicated the fissure had been crudely enlarged from a small natural fault.

Linc clambered through the gold objects and entered the fissure. Slade, holding up the torch, followed, catching a glimpse of a jagged, glittering line in the gouged-out rock.

"The vein," Linc said, his voice suddenly hoarse.

He reached out, touched the gleaming streak in the rock, then bent over, picked up a stone from the base of the wall.

Slade, thinking the stone was an ore specimen, leaned forward to look at it—at the last instant, seeing the glare of hate blazing from Linc's eyes, he realized the stone was intended as a weapon.

At the same moment flame from the brush torch sent pain searing through his hand—and from the cave's entrance the youth, Lalo, called—

"Senores! Vengan aqui, pronto! Que vienen Indios—muchos Indios—desde abajo—"

As Linc whirled, his left elbow knocking the Colt aside, right hand swinging the rock toward Slade's head—as the flaming torch dropped from Slade's hand—the meaning of the Spanish words flashed through his mind—

Indians—many Indians—from below—

Chapter 8

Slade warded off Linc's rock-clutching fist with his forearm and chopped the Colt across the yellow hair.

Outside, Tio Luis stood at the edge of the slope looking into the canyon.

"Indians?" Slade said, licking his scorched fingers. "Where?"

The old man pointed with his stump-bandaged hand. Slade squinted into the heat-shimmering air, made out a long line of what looked like insects far below. He started to count, quit when he got to thirty.

"How do you know they're Indians?" he asked. "Maybe they're soldiers. Soldados?"

The old man shook his head.

"No soldados. Indios. Seri. De Isla Tiburon. Malo. Peligroso. Matan gente—y comen."

Slade sorted it out. Seri Indians from Tiburon —that meant shark—Island. Bad. Dangerous. Matar was to kill, comer to eat. They kill people— and eat. Cannibals.

"Let's get the hell out of here."

The old man looked doubtful, pointed toward the side canyon they had come up, said something Slade couldn't understand.

"What? Speak slower. Despacio."

Tio Luis spoke again, more slowly. Slade still didn't understand.

"Says they'll spot our tracks down at the water-hole, cut us off."

Turning, Slade found Linc behind them, swaying slightly, blood seeping through the yellow hair.

The youth, Lalo, tossed a brief questioning phrase at his uncle. The old man's face brightened. He spoke, Linc interpreted—

"Says thar's another way, higher up the canyon. Maybe we can get across while they're tracking us up here."

"Let's go," said Slade, starting toward the trail. But Linc hung back, looked toward the cave.

"Lot of gold in thar."

Slade wondered how many gold objects it would take to pay off Brent Marshall back in Lexington.

But the gold wouldn't do him any good if the Seri caught them.

"Vamanos, senores," called Tio Luis, already heading down the trail.

"Forget the gold," Slade told Linc. "Let's get going."

But Linc turned and strode back toward the cave. Slade shrugged, started after Tio Luis and Lalo. Linc's man, Mono, after a glance back at the cave, followed him.

Linc, leaning far forward to balance the bulky sack on his back, caught up with them at the head of the side canyon. Here they left the faint trail, bore left along the narrow shoulder skirting the base of the cliffs.

Slade dropped behind Linc, to keep an eye on him. Tio Luis led the way, carrying Linc's rifle, wearing his gunbelt. Lalo followed him, Mono's gunbelt around his waist, the horsethief's rifle in one hand, Tio Luis's muzzle loader in the other. Mono scurried along ahead of Linc.

The sun was high now, and descending a long ridge into the upper end of the canyon was like marching into a blast furnace.

Linc, burdened byhis sack of gold, was sweating like a washy horse. His gray shirt was soaked black, his yellow hair hung damp and lank over his neck. As they crossed the bottom of the canyon, headed up the steep slopes toward the high mesa, the big man suddenly halted and dropped the clanking sack to the ground.

"Why the hell am ah carryin' this?" he said. "Ho—Mono—lleva este saco!"

A rebellious look clouded the whiskery, chimp-like face of the little man—the name Mono—monkey—suited him, Slade thought. But when Linc stepped toward him, fist raised, Mono hoisted the bag to his back, started to struggle uphill with it.

Halfway to the top they stopped to catch their breath. Tio Luis climbed on a boulder, lay flat, surveyed the lower canyon.

"Que pasa," Slade asked. He couldn't understand the rapid-fire reply. Again Linc translated.

"They've cut our trail. Half are followin' it, the others are still comin' upcanyon."

They continued the climb, up a ridge, until

about a quarter of a mile from the top came to an extremely steep, shale-covered slope.

In the loose footing Slade slipped back one step for every two he took. Sweat seeped from the soaked band of his hat and ran down his face; salt stung his eyes. He slipped, went to his knees, the carbine banging hard against a rock, recovered and struggled on.

Linc, seeming to have a knack for keeping his balance in the treacherous footing, passed Lalo and Tio Luis near the top, hoisted himself up a final chest-high embankment and looked back.

"Hurry up," he yelled. "They've seen us."

Tio Luis reached the top, and Lalo. But just ahead of Slade, Mono staggered under the bulky, gold-crammed bag. A few strides short of the rim the little man sank to his knees, letting the sack rest on the ground.

"Peso mucho," he groaned as Slade came up beside him.

Linc cut loose a burst of Spanish from above. Mono ducked his shoulder under the bag and Slade helped him up, supporting him with one hand as the little man stumbled uphill.

Linc reached down, grabbed the sack, and swung it onto the embankment.

Hearing shouts from below, Slade looked back. Several pursuers, men in tattered pants and shirts, were already climbing the shale-covered slope. Strung out behind were ten or fifteen more. Only a few had guns—long-barreled rifles. Others had sturdy bows and bundles of arrows, spears, clubs, machetes.

Slade hoisted himself atop the embankment, lay flat and squirmed around just in time to see a puff of yellow-white smoke appear at the muzzle of one of the Seri's rifles.

Mono, leaning exhausted against the embankment, gave a strangled cry. Surprise and fear came over his symian features. He reached up, hands groping for the top of the bank. Then he slumped, slowly turned, began to roll downhill. Rolled faster and faster, arms and legs flopping, hat flying off, blood spurting from a gaping wound in his back.

Slade laid his cheek against the stock of the carbine. One of the Seri had paused to reload his rifle. Slade squeezed off a shot. Missed. Probably high—hadn't allowed enough for the downhill trajectory.

Working the trigger-guard loading lever, he aimed at the Indian's feet, squeezed the trigger again—but it wouldn't squeeze.

The carbine had jammed, likely because of the jolt he'd given it coming up the hill. As he worked to clear it, he heard Tio Luis and Lalo banging away with rifles on each side of him.

Then a new note joined the percussion chorus— the sharp, repetitive crack of a revolver.

Linc Weaver, lying prone, had lifted the pistol from his gunbelt around the old man's waist and was squeezing off carefully aimed shots.

Slade jerked his Colt from its holster. For a moment he considered turning the gun on Linc, taking that revolver back. But the Seri were advancing up the slope—

Linc's gun barked. It was an Army Colt, bigger and heavier than Slade's Navy, .44 caliber against .36. Still—

"You'll never hit anything at this range," Slade yelled.

"Gives 'em something to think about," Linc replied. He reached over to extract fresh cartridges from the gunbelt and reloaded the revolver. "An shootin' downhill—"

Resting the long barrel on his left fist, he sighted—fired—

"Eeeyahh!" he shouted. "Tol' ya."

One of the Seri, clutching his shoulder, lurched back down the slope.

"Lucky shot," Slade said. But he leveled his Colt, thumbed the hammer, aimed slightly over the head of the foremost Indian—a taller man than the others, apparently the leader—and fired.

The slug kicked up shale about five yards short.

But after four more shots, the last of which splattered rock at his feet—and after Tio Luis had picked off another Indian with his rifle—the tall Seri called out something and the entire party withdrew down the hill. Out of range, they gathered in a loose group, squatting and gesturing.

Slade turned his Colt toward Linc.

"I'll take that gun now."

But the big man brought his own weapon up.

"Hell you will. Ah was countin'. You fired five shots. You're empty."

Slade resisted the impulse to look at his gun.

"It's got six chambers."

"You don't keep a live shell under yore

hammer.''

"I do when I'm hunting horsethieves."

Linc's face reddened. Slade stared straight into the light blue eyes, challenging Linc to call his bluff.

"Ah think you're empty."

Slowly, deliberately, Slade cocked the Colt.

"Do you?"

The big man returned his stare, furrows creasing his forehead. Slade focused his attention on the large thumb resting on the hammer of the heavy Army Colt. If that thumb moved, ever so slightly—

His eyes measured the distance. Twelve feet? Fifteen? Could he cross that gap before Linc cocked his revolver and fired?

The voice of Tio Luis broke the stalemate.

"Senores—ya vienen otra vez los Indios."

The Seri came more slowly this time, spread out in a well-spaced line. Smoke puffs appeared at gun muzzles, slugs thudded into the bank. As Linc, Tio Luis and Lalo returned the fire, Slade reloaded his revolver, then set to work again on the jammed carbine. With the point of his Bowie he managed to pry a crimped casing loose, permitting another cartridge to click into place.

Poking the barrel over the bank, laying jawbone against stock, Slade was sighting on a Seri when someone else's bullet knocked him down. He fired at the next man over; missed. But his next shot winged a man. Then he hit the tallest Seri squarely in the knee. He sprawled, sliding downhill in the loose shale.

The middle of the Indian line fell back, but the

flanks kept advancing. On the left, Slade saw that several had almost reached the final enbankment. Once they got to the top, the Seri could circle around and cut them off. The same thing would happen on the other flank.

How to stop them? Firepower wouldn't do it, they were nearly out of range.

Looking back, wondering if they should retreat before it was too late, Slade's eyes fell on Linc's gold-filled bag.

Leaping to his feet, he grabbed the sack, dragged it to the edge, and flung it out over the embankment.

Landing twenty yards down the slope, the bag split open, spewing out gold objects in all directions.

Linc leaped to his feet with an outraged howl.

"You fool!" he yelled, swinging his gun toward Slade.

Slade was raising his own gun when a figure appeared between them.

"No senores!" Tio Luis cried. "Ya vamos, mientras los Indios estan ocupado."

He pointed downhill to where the Seri were scrabbling over shale and rocks. Shouts from those below had attracted the Indians on the flanks, who ran toward the still bouncing, skittering objects that glittered in the midday sun.

But not all the Seri were chasing after gold.

Tio Luis lurched suddenly, staggered backward as the boom of one of the Indians' ancient weapons reached them from below.

The old man clutched at his left shoulder.

Crouching, he sidled away from the canyon rim, straightened, and looked down at blood seeping through the fingers of his right hand.

Slade stepped forward to inspect the wound, but Tio Luis shook his head and moved away.

"Es nada," he said. "Vamanos!"

And turning, he led the way toward the trees. After a couple of hundred yards he swung north, parallel to the canyon rim. Half an hour later Slade heard a welcoming nicker as they emerged from the pines into the small meadow where they'd left Lady and the mule.

While Lalo saddled their mounts, Slade looked at the old man's shoulder. There was only one hole, in front. The bullet was still inside. Blood oozed slowly as Slade probed, trying to locate the slug. He couldn't feel it—must be pretty deep. Getting his spare shirt from his saddlebag, he tore off strips to bandage the wound.

He had to help the old man mount the mule. He was swinging into his own saddle when he suddenly realized Linc had disappeared.

"El gringo grande," he said to Tio Luis. "Ha visto?"

The old man shook his head. "Es posible," he said, "los otros caballos—"

Of course. Linc had gone after the other horses. After Prince.

"Where?" Slade asked. "Donde?"

Tio Luis exchanged rapid-fire Spanish with his nephew and pointed south.

"Alla—no muy lejos."

Slade kicked his left foot out of the stirrup so

Lalo could mount behind him and set Lady off at a fast trot in the direction the youth indicated— roughly southwest.

As they rode, Slade, reins in his teeth, worked on the carbine, finally clearing the jam. Then he kept it across the saddlebow, on the alert for Indians. But he saw no sign of them, heard nothing— which only made him more apprehensive. He'd learned during the war that enemies unseen are more dangerous than enemies seen.

After not quite an hour they reached a large meadow. On its far side was a small spring-fed pond. Three horses were picketed within ropes-length of the water. Slade saw at a glance that none of them was Prince.

Chapter 9

So the trail hadn't ended, after all, back there at the mine, Slade thought as Lalo slid down from Lady's back, showing them where two saddles were still concealed in the brush. Linc had come back here, thrown his rig on Prince and ridden off.

Which way?

Not east, certainly. Indians that way, and Linc had only a sixgun, with no spare cartridges, unless he'd had a box in his saddlebags.

That left south, west or north.

It turned out, when they found Prince's hoofprints with that crimped hind shoe, to be slightly west of north.

They followed; Lalo mounted on one of the horses Linc had left behind, Slade and the youth each with another on a lead rope. The old man rode in front, picking out the trail, Lalo next, Slade in the rear.

It was easy going at first, as Linc had started out at a full gallop, and the trail was plain. But after something over a mile he had pulled Prince down to a trot, and later a walk, and the hoofprints became harder to follow. Several times they lost the trail completely in expanses of matted pine needles and, later, grassy meadows, and had to fan out and ride slowly until someone spotted the colt's distinctive track again.

Slade had been so engrossed in following Linc, it wasn't until he noticed Lalo casting apprehensive glances behind that he realized they, too, might be pursued—by the Seri. Or would the Indians give up the chase, now that they'd gotten the gold back?

It was a hopeful thought, but one he didn't have a great deal of confidence in. From that point on he, too, frequently twisted in the saddle to scan their backtrail.

But as miles fell behind, the hope grew that the Seri had, indeed, gathered up their gold and taken it back to the cave on Picacho del Diablo.

The mountain itself, for some time visible through gaps in the trees, disappeared as they descended a gradual western slope. The evergreens thinned out; became interspersed with oak.

In midafternoon they came to a faint but definite trail; saw that Prince's hoofprints followed it almost due north. On the sometimes overgrown but always discernible trail they were able to go faster, alternating at quarter-hour intervals between fast walk and trot.

Shadows were lengthening when they reached the arroyo with a running stream at the bottom. It looked to Slade like a good place to camp for the night. But after they had watered the horses, drank themselves and topped off canteens, Tio Luis said, "Vamos adelante."

The sun had disappeared, ushering in the long upland twilight, when they came to a broad, almost flat meadow. Near its center stood what looked like some kind of fortification—low mounds of dirt surrounded by a stone wall. As they drew closer Slade saw that the earthworks were crumbling 'dobe walls, identified when Tio Luis announced, "Mission San Pedro Martir."

The trail they'd been following continued on past the ruins, and so, Slade saw, did Prince's tracks. But Tio Luis turned his mule in through a gap in the wall.

"Aqui quedamos la noche," he said, and passed some further words with Lalo. As he concluded, his voice faltered, and he swayed in the saddle. When he dismounted, the old man's knees sagged momentarily, but he straightened, pointing toward a corner of the enclosure where the 'dobe mounds stood highest.

"Los caballos alla," he directed.

While he helped Lalo unsaddle, Slade wondered. Keeping their mounts in the most sheltered section of the enclosure, where there was scant grass, instead of in the lush meadow—camping in the fort-like ruins, instead of near the stream in the arroyo—were these only prudent precautions? Or did Tio Luis believe—?

When the horses and mule were picketed, Slade walked over to where the old man sat on a sloping shelf of dirt against the south wall and asked—

"Crea que vienen los Indios?"

Tio Luis looked down at the rifle across his legs and started to shrug, wincing with pain.

"Es posible."

Lalo had gone out into the meadow to cut tall grass and brush as extra feed for the animals.

Taking the old man's machete, Slade went to help him. They had a good supply, and were carrying it back into the enclosure, when they heard a shot.

Dropping his armload of fodder, Slade ran to where Tio Luis, crouching behind the wall, was shoving another cartridge into the firing chamber of Linc's rifle.

"Que pasa?" he asked.

"Un Indio, creo."

Cautiously Slade looked out over the wall. He saw nothing but grassy meadow rimmed with trees.

"Donde?"

"El pino alto." Tio Luis motioned with the rifle toward a tall tree set back from the edge of the clearing.

Eyes probing the growing gloom, Slade could detect no human shape—for that matter, no sign of life whatsoever. Not even a squirrel, of which they'd seen many in this high, wooded country. Not even a bird, and these, too, had been numerous—especially jays and woodpeckers.

But now all was still. Had the rifle shot frightened the wild life? Or the presence of men, here where man had so long been absent? Or were Indians infiltrating the pines, stealthily surrounding them?

Maybe there'd been only one Indian. Maybe it hadn't been the Seri, merely some lone hunter. Maybe there'd been no one. Maybe the old man, wounded, exhausted, had only imagined he saw movement near the tall tree.

They had a cold, meager meal. Linc Weaver had taken all of his party's food. Of the supplies Tio

Luis and Slade had brought only a small amount of the dried, shredded meat and a quarter-sack of cornmeal remained, to be shared now between three instead of two. Their dinner, as portioned out by the old man, consisted of a skimpy handful of the meat and slightly larger handful of meal apiece.

Slade was washing the last of the cornmeal down with a swallow of tepid water when the stillness was broken by a distant rolling, rumbling roar.

Thunder, was his first thought, but the fast-darkening sky was cloudless.

"What—?"

"Un derrumbe," Tio Luis said. "De piedras, en el picacho. Creo que los Indios han cerrado la cueva."

Slade wasn't familiar with "derrumbe." But the sound of the word, with the rolling Spanish double R, gave a hint. And piedras were rocks. The old man believed the Seri had triggered a new rockslide on Picacho del Diablo, to re-close the mouth of the treasure cave.

Now that they had closed the cave, would the Seri set out in force to overtake the intruders? Was the Indian Tio Luis had shot at an advance scout, sent to trail the fugitives? Was he backtracking now to lead the main body to the ruined mission?

Time held the answers. All they could do was watch and wait—it was already too dark to travel. Perhaps when the moon rose—but that would be some hours. And the old man—

"Come esta?" Slade asked.

"Bien," was the reply. "Estoy bien."

But the shaky huskiness of his voice contradicted

the words. Below the wound, his shirt was sodden with blood.

"Let's have another look at that," Slade said, reaching to unbutton the shirt.

Tio Luis jerked away from him and turned to peer over the wall. He growled something over his shoulder. Picking out two phrases, "Duerman ustedes" and "Yo quedo vigia," Slade understood him to mean he and Lalo should sleep while the old man kept watch. Turning the words back on him, Slade said—

"No hombre. Usted duerma—yo quedo vigia."

But Tio Luis ignored him.

Slade crossed the enclosure to the place where the horses and mule were picketed. Lady moved toward him in the near-dark. He stroked her nose as she laid her head against his chest and patted the swell of her shoulder. Getting a soft cloth from a saddle bag, he rubbed the mare down. When he was finished he returned the cloth to the saddlebag and slumped down with his back to the sloping 'dobe, the carbine beside him.

If the old man insisted on watching for Indians, he'd guard the horses.

Overhead, stars spread across the sky, glistening in crystal-ink clarity of thin, dry air. Air now quite cold. Slade pulled Lady's saddlecloth over him. The horse-sweat smell of it reminded him of the stables at Shelbourne Farm, and of bivouacs on hot July nights in Kentucky with John Morgan's raiders.

He was awakened by Lalo's hand clutching his shoulder; the youth's voice, hushed but urgent, in his ear.

"Senor—Tio Luis esta muy enfermo."

The old man lay on his back on the 'dobe shelf, rifle by his side. His eyes stared upward, reflecting starglow. At first Slade thought he was dead, then the chest heaved in a slow spasm. As the old man exhaled, a half-strangled moan escaped through gritting teeth. Slade put a hand on his forehead, found it fiery hot.

Pouring a little water from a canteen into his cupped hand, he bathed the old man's face, repeating the process several times. Gradually the labored breathing eased, the eyes lost their fixed stare. But just when Slade thought the crisis was passed, he became aware of a clicking sound. The old man's teeth were chattering. He began to tremble—to shake more and more violently—

"Blankets," Slade told Lalo. "Get blankets." he groped for a Spanish word and came up with, "sarapes—pronto!"

Lalo disappeared into the darkness and returned with two threadbare blankets. Slade threw them over the shaking body, tucked them under and resumed bathing the old man's face.

Gradually the shivering eased, Tio Luis's eyes closed and he fell asleep. Slade went to his bedroll, got his own two English wool blankets and substituted them for the others.

He handed Linc's rifle to Lalo, motioning for him to keep watch. Then he sat, back against the stone wall, to keep an eye on the old man. Wished he had a cigarette, remembered the last of his tobacco was inside the bandana-bandage on Tio

Luis's stump-finger.

Listening to the old man's still-labored breathing, he wondered what to do. The fever was down some now, but it would go up again. The only chance to save Tio Luis would be to dig that slug out of his shoulder. But as deep as it was in, he couldn't go probing around with his knife in the dark. And there should be hot water to sterilize the knife, cleanse the wound.

But hot water meant a fire, and a fire might be a beacon to guide the Seri to them through the night. Was the added risk to three lives worth it, to possibly save one?

Maybe later, when the moon rose, there'd be light enough to do something about that shoulder.

And light enough for an Indian attack?

The shape under the blankets moved, the old man gave a low moan. Slade dampened his face again. Then, taking up his carbine, he rose and looked over the wall.

Gazing out over the clearing, he became aware for the first time of how much light the stars provided. Looking up, he saw that the eastern part of the sky was shiny gray-white, very much like a fine lace shawl his grandmother had worn for show, not warmth, on long-ago summer evenings at Shelbourne Farm.

This broad, glittering band—the Milky Way—and myriad other pinpoints suffusing the blue-black infinity cast a silvery sheen over the meadow surrounding the mission.

But beyond the borders of the clearing, trees threw deep shadows. As Slade's eyes probed fruitlessly into those shadows, the feeling grew inside him that there was life out there.

Animal life, certainly. Perhaps deer—several times they'd glimpsed a small, stunted variety through the trees. Once a band of antelope had raced across a distant slope. And only that afternoon, pointing to claw marks on a fallen tree, Tio Luis had called out, "Oso"—bear.

And always coyote, heard howling at night, occasionally seen in the daytime skulking through the brush.

Was there human life out there, also?

What if the Seri had sent not one advance scout, but two? Or several? Were they concealed in the tree-shrouded gloom, watching?

Slade's fingers tightened on the carbine. His eyes strained; seemed to detect a flicker of movement where that tall tree Tio Luis had pointed out earlier towered against the dark night. His ears, too, seemed to pick up faint sounds from that direction.

Animal sounds? Or human sounds?

Assuming Indians wouldn't advertise their presence, maybe animal sounds.

Or was it only his over-active imagination?

Another moan drew his attention back to the form on the ground. Again he bathed the old man's face.

"Esta muy enfermo, senor—verdad?"

He had almost forgotten Lalo, standing a little beyond the old man's feet, his elbows resting on the wall, the rifle in his hands.

"Si—es verdad," Slade said.

It certainly was true—the old man was very sick.

"Crea usted," the youth asked, "que mi tio va a morir?"

"Dios sabe," Slade replied, using a phrase he had heard often since entering once-Spanish territory.

God knew, but Slade had strong suspicions—suspicions confirmed when, about halfway between the appearance of the waning moon and the first light of dawn, Tio Luis breathed his last.

Chapter 10

It was a soft, sighing, shuddering exhalation.

"Esta muerto," Lalo said, husky-voiced.

Slade nodded.

He felt guilty, now, that he hadn't done more to try and save Tio Luis. Risked a fire, for light, and to heat water—tried to dig the bullet out with his knife. Or made the attempt later, by moonlight. But with that fever—having lost so much blood— such crude surgery would certainly have killed him anyway.

He reached out, brushed the eyelids closed, drew one of the blankets over the already waxy-looking head.

Lalo was mumbling in Spanish—doubtless prayers. Slade bowed his own head for some moments, then rose, took up his carbine and looked over the wall.

The moon, well into its last quarter, didn't add greatly to the light from the stars. The silver sheen over the clearing was slightly brighter, but the shadows under the trees were dark by contrast.

Later, Slade again thought he heard sounds from the vicinity of the tall pine. Still later, while looking toward another part of the meadow, from the corner of his eye he sensed a flicker of motion near the base of that tree. But when he looked directly at it, all was still.

Yet as dawn paled the eastern sky, the impression grew that he had seen something. When color heralded the sun, by sign and word—the word the old man had used the night before, "vigia"—Slade told Lalo to keep a lookout. Crossing the mission enclosure, he scaled the stone wall opposite the tall pine, trotted to the woods, cautiously circled the meadow.

Among the other trees, he couldn't see the big pine. When he thought he was getting close he slowed, finally halted—listened—

Took a cautious step and froze as raucous squawks broke out overhead. Looking up, he saw an angrily scolding drab-blue jay.

Scolding? Or warning?

If there were Seri nearby—

Holding the carbine ready, he moved slowly forward. After a final outburst, the jay flapped off.

Rounding a squatty juniper, Slade saw the tall pine. As he drew closer he made out something on the ground half a dozen yards beyond the rough-barked trunk. A man-sized something.

Throwing the carbine to his shoulder, thumbing back the hammer, he sighted on the object—held his breath.

When the object remained motionless for more than a minute he resumed his advance until he was close enough to be sure the man-sized something was—a man.

A few more steps and he lowered the carbine.

There would be no danger from this man.

Tio Luis's single bullet had done its work. Now Slade understood the sounds he'd heard during the night. The sounds of animals feeding on fresh-killed flesh. On the soft, tender parts—genitals, buttocks, belly and interior organs.

Clothing had been ripped to blood-soaked shreds. But crude sandals, dark skin, and black hair, indicated the victim was an Indian. A scout for the Seri. Thanks to Tio Luis's accuracy with the rifle, this Indian hadn't carried word back to the main party. But when he didn't return, others would set out on his trail.

Slade wheeled and trotted quickly to the ruins.

"Come on," he called to Lalo as he vaulted over a low spot in the wall. "Let's get out of here before the Seri come."

Though he spoke in English, the youth seemed to understand. He looked down questioningly at the still form under the blanket.

Slade pondered the problem. They couldn't bury the old man here. The ground was too hard and they had no digging tools. There were plenty of loose stones around, from crumbling sections of the wall. A rock cairn would protect the corpse from animals—but reveal it to the Seri. They would surely mutilate it—or worse.

But to take the body home to the rancho meant several days in the low-country heat.

Maybe they should take it with them—when they were safe from pursuit, bury it.

Sunlight was filtering through the treetops when they rode away from the ruins of the mission, continuing along the trail they had followed the day before.

Lalo rode in front, leading the mule, to which Tio Luis's blanket-shrouded body was lashed. Slade rode behind on Lady, with the two other horses on lead ropes.

As they reached the edge of the meadow Slade looked over his shoulder and saw three buzzards swooping in descending circles around the tall pine.

He cursed the carrion eaters. They'd guide the Seri more quickly to the body of their fallen tribesman.

"Andale, joven," he called ahead to the youth.

But when Lalo kicked his mount into a lope the body of Tio Luis jounced so wildly on the mule that Slade, afraid it would fall off, shouted, "No joven—cuidado—despacio."

So they proceeded at a fast walk as the trail trended northwest and down until, at the beginnings of an arroyo, it swung west. About a mile down the arroyo they came to a rock-catchment pool where they hastily watered the horses and topped off their canteens.

As they continued, Slade kept an anxious eye on their backtrail, constantly expecting to see Indians —or worse, to not see them but suddenly feel the impact of bullet or arrow.

But as the sun grew higher and hotter, as they made steady progress downward, leaving the pines behind, passing through manzanita and oak and increasingly heavy chaparral, he began to hope.

Maybe the Seri wouldn't follow them, after all. Maybe they weren't that interested in avenging the death of their scout. Maybe they wouldn't press the pursuit into the lowlands. After all, they were a long way from home. And they'd gotten back their gold. Maybe—

Maybe you're a dreaming, wool-gathering damn fool, Shelbourne, he told himself, swinging around in his saddle, one hand on Lady's smooth, sweat-damp rump, to carefully inspect every bush, scrubby tree and boulder behind them.

Maybe, he thought, *we should have left the old man's body there at the mission—kind of an appeasement to the Seri—*

He broke that thought off as he remembered the Seri were said to be cannibals.

Still, having the body along was slowing them up. Slade began to spend less time watching the backtrail and more looking for a place to bury Tio Luis.

The sun was blazing down from dead overhead before he found one.

By this time they were well down in the foothills. This trail was less steep and hazardous than the one to the north that he and Tio Luis had used as a shortcut to the high country.

The arroyo they were descending became wider, its bottom more sand than rock. Sand tended to collect particularly below the occasional bends. Slade could imagine, when high country rains filled the arroyo, back-eddies below the bends piling up sand against the dirt banks while carving those banks into steep, swirling contours.

It was below one of these banks, with a thick bed of loose sand at its base, that they buried Tio Luis.

Scooping out sand with their hands to a depth of better than two feet, they laid the blanket-shrouded body in the bottom. It had stiffened considerably lying over the back of the mule, and they couldn't straighten it out completely, so they laid it on its side, bent slightly at the waist.

They covered the body with sand, then, with branches torn from a nearby bush, gouged away at the overhanging bank until it collapsed, covering the grave with another couple of feet of soil.

They smoothed out the ground around the grave with more branches, hoping that if the Seri were following, they wouldn't notice it. Then, picketing the three spare horses—Lalo switched his saddle to the mule—they ate a hasty meal.

But when they were ready to leave, Lalo walked over to the grave, making new tracks across the smoothed-over sand.

Slade started to ask what the hell the youth thought he was doing, but bit down on the words as Lalo sank to his knees beside the grave.

Picking up one of the loose branches, Slade walked over and stood beside him.

"I'm sorry," he said. "Lo siento. Your uncle was a fine man. Buen hombre." He laid his hand on the youth's shoulder.

Lalo looked up. There was a hint of moisture about the dark eyes and his voice was thick as he said, quite distinctly—"Thank you, senor."

"You speak English?" Slade said, startled.

"Pretty good," said Lalo. "I learn in school when we live in San Diego."

"But why didn't you say so before?" Slade

thought of the trouble he'd gone through having Linc translate Tio Luis's Spanish.

The youth looked down at the grave. "Tio Luis say, a man learn much when others don't know he understand."

Then why, Slade wondered, are you telling me now?

He recalled his doubts about Lalo. Ever since he and Tio Luis had caught up with Linc and his party, he had wondered about that days-ago "Abajo los Yanquis" shout.

Could he trust the youth now?

"Come on," he said, tightening his grip on Lalo's shoulder. "We'd best be moving."

But it was already too late.

Slade was smoothing out the last footprints, backing away from the grave, when small geysers of sand began spurting up around him. It wasn't until he heard the multiple boom of guns that he realized what caused the sand-spurts.

He whirled, looked up the arroyo.

They were coming down a ridge, less than a quarter-mile away. About twenty of them. Several with rifles, crouched, reloading.

Slade made a dash for Lady, from the corner of his eye seeing Lalo leap onto the mule.

Slade's backside hit the saddle, his boot heels banged Lady's sides. The mare started with a great bound just as another volley of shots rang out and off to the left a horse—one of the picketed extra horses—screamed in pain.

The horse went down, thrashing, blood spouting from its shoulder. The other two, unhurt, lunged and reared, trying to pull their picket stakes.

Slade swung Lady toward them, but Lalo yelled—

"No senor! Leave them!"

As more shots rang out, Slade decided that was good advice. He heeled Lady's ribs, sent her charging after the youth on his mule.

Moments later, looking over his shoulder, he saw the first Seri reach the downed horse and with one swing of his machete slash its neck open below the throatlatch.

Sounds of gunfire mingling in his ears with the drumming of hoofs, Slade crouched low over Lady's neck. Quickly the mare swept past Lalo's much slower mule.

When he was sure they were beyond range of the Indians' venerable firearms, Slade tightened rein, pulled Lady down to a rocking canter. Looking back again, he saw the Seri clustered around the horses.

The arroyo curved around a low hill. Slade slowed Lady to a walk, sent her back up the far side of the hill. From its crest he could see that the Indians were still bunched around the horses. The flash of knives in the sun told him the Seri were butchering the dead horse.

Hoofs crunched on the rocky soil as Lalo rode up beside him.

"I no think they follow now," the youth said. "I think they eat."

"Vamanos anyway," Slade said. "They might change their minds."

After a couple of miles at an easy canter, and a

couple more at a walk, Slade reined up. Looking back, he could see no sign of pursuit. Apparently Lalo was right, the Seri were going to feast on dead horse.

He swung down from the saddle. "Let's give 'em a rest," he said to Lalo, easing Lady's cinch.

While their mounts nibbled ineffectually, bits still in place, at brush and dried grass growing alongside the arroyo, Slade looked for sign of Linc Weaver and Prince. But though he searched the sandy bottom of the arroyo and the ground for some distance to each side, he found no prints of a shod horse. In fact, he found no indication of the trail they had been following down from the heights.

"Where's the trail?" he asked Lalo. And when the youth replied that this was the trail, here in the arroyo, Slade objected—

"But there are no tracks of el gringo grande—with my horse."

Lalo looked puzzled, then his face brightened. About five miles back, he explained, before they reached the place where they buried Tio Luis, the trail forked. One fork followed the arroyo, the other branched southwest leading to an old rancho, now deserted. Probably, he said, Linc had taken the other fork.

Slade looked back. Because of the Seri, they couldn't backtrack to pick up Linc's trail. Better to keep going, hope to find his tracks on the main trail going north. They might even reach the trail ahead of him, catch him coming up from the south.

They remounted and started off. The going was easier now. They were out of the foothills, on a broad, flat benchland that sloped gently toward the sea. As the arroyo began to meander in ever-widening loops across the plain they quit following it, struck straight for the coast, though still crossings its sandy bed occasionally.

In late afternoon at one of these crossings, where green shrubs and small trees lined the bank, they dug down into the sand and refilled their canteens. Then they continued on toward the lowering sun.

They reached the main trail before Slade expected it. Still some miles from the coast, with a line of low hills in front of them, and to the north the white gleam of sand dunes bordering the sea.

Though not wide, the trail was distinct. A dusty pathway, worn down a couple of inches below the surrounding ground.

Clearly outlined in the loose surface were the hoofprints of a shod horse—with a crimped hind shoe. Linc was still ahead of them.

They followed the trail until dark; made a dry, fireless camp. Slade decided not to try to travel by night. The moon was now too far gone, rising only an hour or so before dawn.

The next morning Prince's hoofprints on the trail had been blurred by a light overnight dew. The sun was high overhead before the prints became sharp again.

They were half a day behind.

That night they camped at the rocky tinajas where Slade had made the decision to take the shortcut into the mountains. The next night was another dry camp, and the following morning, starting out when it was still dark, with a final sliver of moon fading in the eastern sky, Lalo said he thought they'd reach the rancho in the arroyo by noon.

Slade wondered which he was going to enjoy most, a long drink of cool water from the well, or a meal of Coco's excellent cooking.

They'd had little to drink along the way, and less to eat. The animals had to subsist on mesquite branches Lalo cut for them each night, and whatever dried, straggly, leaf-like vegetation they managed to crop. As for Slade and Lalo, they had choked down the last of the cornmeal crumbs the morning before, and that night had sucked on the pulpy interior of prickly pear cactus leaves that Lalo peeled with Slade's knife.

As they rode on through the growing morning heat, Slade also wondered if, from the arroyo rim, he would behold the welcome sight of Prince again in that small cactus corral beside the ranchhouse.

But when, with the sun a little past its zenith, they did reach the rim of the broad arroyo, a totally unexpected sight greeted his eyes.

He had forewarning that something was amiss. Lalo, recognizing familiar landmarks, had hurried ahead. Not wanting to extend Lady any more than necessary, Slade lagged behind. But when he heard the cry that escaped the youth's lips, Slade urged the mare into a fast trot.

Reining up beside Lalo, who had halted his mule, the first thing Slade noticed was that the windmill was down. Its rickety tower had been toppled over, the rough-hewn poles that formed it torn apart and scattered.

Then he saw that the house, though its walls still stood, had been reduced to a 'dobe shell. Dark scorch marks around the top of the walls indicated that thatch-and-pole roof had been destroyed by fire. So had the roof and supports of the lean-to kitchen in back, and the ramada across the front.

With another anguished cry, Lalo whipped his mule with the end of the reins and sent him galloping down the sloping trail. Slade followed at a more cautious pace, realizing that haste was useless. No hint of smoke rose from the ruins. The fire was long since out—whatever happened had taken place many hours, probably days, before.

Reinforcing this impression, as he rode toward the 'dobe shell a sickish-sweetish odor assaulted his nostrils, a smell reminiscent of wartime battlefields —the stench of death.

Rounding the corner of the house, Slade found Lalo sitting his mule, facing the front doorway, staring down with horrified expression at three forms lined up on the ground before it.

Three fire-scorched, sun-bloated, savagely mutilated naked bodies.

Despite the mutilation, Slade could see that two of the bodies had been males, one female. For a moment a terrible sick feeling went through him as he thought of the girl, Coco. Then he saw gray hair, realized the female body was not just bloated, but heavy to begin with.

This, then, was the wife of the old rancher from up the arroyo. The two once-male bodies must be her husband and their son, who had come to stay with Coco while Tio Luis was gone.

"But where?"

"Your sister—?" he said to Lalo.

As the youth turned toward him, Slade saw that his dark eyes were awash with tears.

"They take her," he said in a hoarse, choking voice.

"They?" said Slade. "Who did this?"

"Indios." Lalo nodded toward the bodies. "Indios kill these—take my sister."

"Indios?" Slade looked across the arroyo to the trail they'd come down. For the past day and a half he'd given scarcely a thought to the Seri, convinced they had abandoned the chase. Was it possible the Indians had passed them on the way?

Lalo, catching the direction of Slade's glance, shook his head.

"No, senor, not Seri." He jerked his head toward the northeast. "These Yuma, from the big river. They come here sometimes to rob and kill—steal women."

"We'll go after them," said Slade, starting to rein Lady around. "Maybe we can catch them—save your sister."

But the youth shook his head.

"No, senor. They are now far away."

"But we have to try. She's your sister—"

Slade broke off, realizing his concern over Coco's fate went far beyond the fact she was Lalo's sister. He remembered the first fever-misted glimpse of her face—the brown eyes with the dark mote. Her gentle hands soothing him, bathing his hot brow, treating his wound. And that last morning as he and Tio Luis set out on the trail south. That final touch of her hand—the look in those brown eyes—her parting smile—

"Come on," he said more urgently. "Let's find their trail—go after them. Vamanos!"

But the youth, tears now etching channels down his dusty cheeks, again shook his head.

"No, senor," he said, his voice thick with emotion. "My sister may be alive, but if we trail Yuma, they see us, they will kill her. Better we don't follow. Maybe somehow—someday—she escape."

"All right," Slade said at last with a shrug of resignation. "We'll go on to San Diego."

Perhaps there, he thought, they could get up a party to go in search of the missing girl. Meanwhile—

His eyes went to the three bloated, mutilated bodies.

They found tools in the wreckage behind the ranchhouse, dug a shallow but wide pit and placed the bodies in it, filled the pit with dirt and covered it with a mound of rocks. Lalo fashioned three crosses from twisted branches and stuck them in among the rocks, from which they projected at irregular angles.

With a scorched kettle tied to a reata they drew water from the well beside the wreckage of the windmill. They replenished their canteens, let lady and the mule drink, drew some more water and made a fire, boiling several handfuls of beans from a small pottery jar the Indians had overlooked under remains of the lean-to kitchen. After cooking more than two hours the beans were still tough and tasteless, but long, determined chewing reduced them to a pulp soft enough to be swallowed.

In the meantime, Lady and the mule had been stripping dust-gray leaves from the immature stalks in the cornfield.

Late in the afternoon they saddled up and climbed the steep, winding trail northward out of the arroyo. At the top they paused to look back. Slade recalled his first glimpse of the little rancho under the broiling sun what seemed such a long time ago. He heard a choked-back sob from Lalo, saw tears again brimming in the youth's eyes before he turned away quickly, dug heels into the mule's ribs.

Not quite two days—and some sixty miles—later, in early afternoon, they passed the mud-wall ruins of an old mission. On up the long valley beyond vineyards and orchards Slade saw the large rancho he had avoided on the trip south.

Now, hunger again wrenching at their bellies, their weary mounts, heads low, proceeding at a shambling walk, there was no thought of detouring around the rancho. On the contrary, it must provide them with food—water—supplies—for the remainder of the journey to San Diego. Even, he thought, if these supplies had to be commandeered, as John Hunt Morgan's raiders commandeered their supplies on the march into Ohio. He drew the carbine from its scabbard, held it across the saddle bow.

As they neared the rancho, a large main structure of whitewashed adobe surrounded by trees, corrals and outbuildings, Lady lifted her head, quickened her step.

Smells water and food, Slade thought. But it was more than that.

Lady's head rose higher, her lips parted, a shrill neigh whistled through her teeth.

An answer came from a corral beside the rancho, and a thrill shivered along Slade's spine as he saw a big blood bay wheel and come toward them.

Warrior Prince!

Then, as he saw Prince's proud head bobbing sharply with each hurried step, Slade's heart plunged and a curse came to his lips.

Prince was lame.

Chapter 11

Beside the corral, Slade swung down from Lady, squirmed between horizontal poles, patted Prince's neck.

"Easy, boy, easy." And as the colt butted his head against his shoulder—"Sure, fella, I'm glad to see you, too. Mighty glad."

Squatting, he ran his hand lightly along the lower left foreleg, then the other leg.

Touch confirmed what his eyes had noticed, a slight but definite swelling on the inside of the left leg, a little below the knee.

Prince had popped a splint—ruptured the membrane sheething the metatarsal, or splint, bone and the cannon, the big lower foreleg bone.

A common injury in young horses subjected to hard usage.

Rest was the best cure. Slade had heard of a technique called "firing"—burning small holes around the infected area, causing irritation that speeded the healing process. But he'd also heard that firing sometimes caused infection.

Out of the question to fire Prince way down here in Baja, no vet nearer than San Diego—and that one probably not qualified for more than worming dogs.

It would have to be left to nature's healer—
time.

How much time?

A couple of months—maybe longer. And the date set for the race in San Diego—the race that would decide the fate of Shelbourne Farm—was September 15th. As near as Slade could figure, less than three weeks away.

Could he get a postponement?

Carter Armstrong, the San Diego banker who was acting as stakeholder and race official, had explained the main provisions of the race agreement, a lengthy document in Spanish. Date, time—5 p.m. to avoid the heat of the day, course—from the Pueblo out the beach road to the end of Point Loma and back.

There had been something about a forfeit clause, but the banker had said it was "only a formality. These people love to draw up long documents— which they don't pay the least attention to."

Slade had suspected the banker was making an oblique reference to the Californios' notorious custom of disregarding their financial obligations. For which, considering the usurious interest rates, he didn't blame them.

As these thoughts went through his head, Slade made a more thorough inspection of Prince, to be sure the splint was his only injury. He ran his hands again over the forelegs, then the hind legs, found no other hot spots. He lifted each foot—the shoes were worn, but there were no stones, no cracks in the hoofs. Ran his hands over withers and back, found a small saddle gall, nothing serious.

He stepped back for a longer range look. Prince was gaunt from much travel and little food, but his coat was good, his eyes clear and alert.

As he finished his inspection, Slade became aware of voices behind him, speaking Spanish. A thought flashed in his mind—Prince was here—was the man who had stolen him here too?

Hand dropping to the butt of his Colt, he whirled, expecting to see big, yellow-haired Linc Weaver.

But the man who stood beside the corral talking with Lalo was of medium height, slender, and dark. Dark hair and eyes, dark, carefully trimmed mustache, though the face under a wide brimmed, flat crowned hat with an openwork silver band was little darker than Slade's own.

Thin lips parted in a grin that revealed shell-white teeth; a glint of amusement lighted the dark eyes as they fixed on Slade's hand, hovering over the gunbutt.

"Don't be alarmed, senor," he said in virtually accentless English—acquired, he told Slade later, as a youth growing up in Santa Barbara—"You are in no danger here."

He stepped forward, extended his hand.

Slade crawled through the bars of the corral, shook the hand.

"Roberto Rodriguez, senor—su servidor."

Slade supplied his own name.

"Bienvenido—welcome to Rancho San Lorenzo." Rodriguez nodded toward Lalo. "The boy tells me that this fine caballo"—with an admiring glance at Prince—"is yours."

Slade confirmed this, adding that the colt had been bred on his family's farm in Kentucky.

"Then I'm afraid I've lost a horse. I believed the big blond man when he said this horse, which had gone lame, was his. I loaned him a horse to continue his journey to San Diego."

"I'll pay you for your horse," said Slade. But Rodriguez shook his head.

"No, senor—I won't take your money. I have many horses—one mas o menos is of no importance."

Then, turning toward the tile-roofed ranch-house—

"But come—you must be hungry. We've just finished comida, but I'll tell the cook to fix a little something for you."

In the cool interior of the house, shielded from mid-afternoon heat by four-foot-thick walls, "a little something" turned out to be copious quantities of barbecued beef, rice, beans and an endless stream of tortillas supplied hot from the stovetop. To wash it down there was a full-bodied red wine— a product, Roberto Rodriguez announced proudly, of San Lorenzo's own winery, from grapevines planted almost a hundred years before by the Dominican padres.

When Slade had eaten his fill—Lalo had been taken off to eat in the kitchen—Rodriguez refilled their glasses and supplied cigars—tightly twisted affairs of almost black tobacco.

Through clouds of blue-gray smoke, in response to his host's questions, Slade told of the theft of Warrior Prince from Rancho Los Robles and his pursuit oi Linc Weaver and his band. He thought it prudent to omit details of the Indian mine and its treasure, but included the encounters with the Seri and the death of Tio Luis.

Then, when he told of the Yuma attack on the rancho in the arroyo—three killed and the girl, Coco, carried off—the slender man banged his fist on the table and rattled off a string of Spanish oaths. He rose and went to the doorway, called. Almost immediately a thickset, round-faced man appeared. After a brief exchange he hurried away again.

"I'm going to send some men," Rodriguez said. "Cross-country—try to pick up the trail—"

Slade got to his feet.

"I'd like to go with them."

Rodriguez shook his head. "It would be better not. My men—they are mostly Indian themselves. They'll take care not to be seen. If it's possible to free the girl, they'll do it."

Slade spent three days at Rancho San Lorenzo. Not from choice. He'd like to have set out immediately on the trail to San Diego—hoping to catch up with Linc Weaver. But Lady needed rest after her long Baja trek. And he wanted to keep an eye on Prince for awhile.

Much of the three days, when he wasn't caring for his horses, he spent riding over the rancho's vast, cactus-covered acreage with Roberto Rodriguez and his vaqueros. He was greatly impressed by the ranchero and his men—the cool, competent way they handled near-wild cattle on the brush-covered, arroyo-carved terrain; their horsemanship—tough, wiry riders perfectly attuned to their tough, agile ponies as they made long sweeps through valleys and over hills.

It was after the longest of these expeditions, an all-day ride westward through a cypress-studded canyon to the sea and back, that Slade decided to leave the next morning for San Diego.

Lady had responded quickly to ample feed, water, and rest. Her head was high and her coat glossy, though her ribs still showed with some prominence.

Prince's progress was less encouraging. The swelling below his knee seemed to have gone down some, but his head still bobbed as he favored the leg while walking. It would obviously be some time before he would be fit to travel.

"Can I leave him with you for a few weeks?" Slade asked Rodriguez that night at supper.

"Certainly," was the reply. "As long as you like. He will have the best of care."

Slade was convinced he would.

There was one other matter on his mind— another reason he had stayed over at Rancho San Lorenzo. He spoke of it just before going to bed.

"Have you heard anything from your men," he asked Rodriguez, "about the girl?"

The ranchero shook his head. "Not yet. It's a long way. It may be some time. And"—he looked down at the floor, then up again—"there's really only a very small chance—"

The sun was just rising above the hills when Slade and Lalo rode up the trail winding northward out of the valley. It was nearing the sea on the evening of the second day following as they skirted marshlands bordering San Diego Bay.

A long, low sandspit culminating in a flat, bight-notched island bordered the bay on the west; a massive headland guarded the entrance on the north.

Near the midpoint of the bayshore they came on row after row of small yellow flags fluttering in the brisk breeze atop yard-high stakes. It was only when Slade recalled a remark overheard soon after his arrival in San Diego that he realized what the flags were—markers for building lots. In the spring a speculator from San Francisco had bought up almost a thousand acres of land here, several miles south of where the town had existed since the coming of the Spaniards.

"Old man Horton's an idiot," a bearded individual standing at the bar of the Franklin House had said. "He'll never sell lots down there—too far up the bay—and no water. This is where the town started—this is where it'll stay."

It looked as though the bearded man had been right. There were hundreds of flags, but only a handful of buildings, including the deserted army barracks built 20 years earlier during a previous abortive attempt to relocate the town.

For that matter, the town itself, which they reached about an hour later, didn't amount to much. Huddled at the base of a low hill was a cluster of mostly 'dobe buildings, mostly one story, grouped rather haphazardly around a bare, dusty rectangle that only for lack of a better word could be called a plaza.

Pausing at the edge of this rectangle, Slade examined it carefully, hand near his gunbutt, half expecting to see the hulking form, the long blond hair, of Linc Weaver.

But the plaza was empty except for a raggedly clad Indian slumped against a wall, empty wine bottle beside him, and nearby a piebald hound scratching hopelessly at his scabby hide.

Slade guided Lady to a long, low building of whitewashed 'dobe that dominated the east side of the plaza. A small wooden cupola topped the red tile roof directly above a wide-arched entrance. This was the town home of Don Ricardo Castillo, owner of Rancho Los Robles, from which Prince had been stolen.

Dismounting, Slade looped Lady's reins around a hitch rail and banged a brass knocker against a metal plate set in one of a pair of massive wooden doors.

After some time the door opened about a foot and a dark face peered out.

"Don Ricardo?" Slade asked.

"Quien le quiere?"

Slade gave his name and the door closed in his face. But a minute later it swung open again—wide open—and Don Ricardo himself greeted him.

"Senor Shelbourne—so good you come back."

Grasping Slade's hand, Castillo crushed it in his. Almost a head shorter than Slade, he was more than a hundred pounds heavier—mostly solid muscle distributed over a bearlike body. In fact he was often called—though not to his face—"El Oso."

"Where have you been?" he asked, leading Slade into a patio enclosed on three sides by the house, on the fourth by a barn and storage sheds. "We looked for you, but we lost the trail. Did you find your horse?"

As Slade replied, "Yes, but—" Don Ricardo raised his hand.

"You must be tired—thirsty. We will have some wine, you can tell us all about it."

He called to a servant. Wine and bread and cheese were brought, and they sat under an arbor in the patio, which in contrast to the plaza in front of the house was filled with flowers, bushes, fruit trees and grapevines. Here they were joined by Don Ricardo's wife, Dona Ysabel, his eldest son, Miguel, and a daughter, Juana.

Dona Ysabel was her husband's exact opposite, a tiny woman whose firm jaw and sharply penetrating dark eyes belied her lack of size.

The son took after his father, short and stocky.

The daughter, 16-year-old Juana, bore little resemblance to either her father or mother. She had cream-gold skin and near-blond hair, heritage of some north-of-Spain ancestor.

When Slade had visited the Castillo house a month before, Juana had seemed a vivacious child. Bigger than the younger children, whose voices he now heard from within the house—almost as tall as her brother Miguel, in fact—but still a child.

But as she dipped before him now in a low curtsy Slade glimpsed beneath the neckline of her rose-pink gown unmistakable evidence that Juana Castillo was no child.

Don Ricardo suggested that his daughter, who spoke English fluently, translate for her mother, who understood little of the language. The girl took a chair near Slade's, and a hint of perfume mingled with the patio's odors of flower and fruit.

Daylight was fading as slade began to tell of his search for Warrior Prince, pausing at intervals while Juana Castillo's soft voice transformed his words into liquid syllables.

Before he finished the sky was black above and servants had lit oil lamps suspended from the outer edges of the roof overhang, bathing the patio in a yellow glow.

"So," said Don Ricardo, refilling the wine glasses and emptying his with one huge swallow, "your caballo is lame. How long before he is better —able to race?"

Slade shrugged. "Two—three months—maybe longer."

Don Ricardo's beefy hand rubbed a thick crop of black sidewhiskers.

"Possibly Don Jose will agree to a delay. I will send for him."

But the messenger he dispatched returned almost immediately—Don Jose Sandoval's imposing two-story house, as near a mansion as the town could boast, was only the width of a narrow street away. Don Jose was not at home. As city treasurer he was attending a meeting at the red brick home of Thomas Whaley, a couple of blocks east.

Don Ricardo sent the messenger back to request that Don Jose come to see him when he returned. Then, turning to Slade—

"You will, of course, stay here with us, Senor Shelbourne." His muscular arms opened wide. "Mi casa es su casa, senor."

The evening meal would be served in about half an hour, he added, summoning a servant to show Slade to his room.

Slade hesitated.

"My mare," he began—

"Has been taken care of," said Don Ricardo. "She is in our barn."

"And the boy who was with me?"

After a brief exchange with the waiting servant, Don Ricardo reported Lalo had gone to stay with an aunt who lived in town.

The servant led Slade to a large room featuring a four-poster bed of gleaming brass. *Amazing*, Slade thought, *the things Yankee hide ships had hauled around the horn to trade to the Californios.* His saddle bags and carbine were on a low stand at the foot of the bed.

Another servant arrived with large pitchers of hot and cold water. Slade stripped and sponged off sweat-caked traildust, scraped a three-day stubble from his jaw and took spare trousers and shirt from his saddlebags.

He had buttoned the trousers and was reaching for the shirt when a knock sounded at the door. Thinking it was a servant calling him for supper, he crossed the room and threw open the door.

Standing there, a flush appearing on her cheeks as she gazed at Slade's half-clothed torso, was Don Ricardo's daughter, Juana.

"Perdoname   senor,"   she   began,   visibly

flustered. But then, switching to English—

"Pardon me—but there is this letter—"

She held out a wrinkled envelope. As he took it, their fingers touched—it seemed to Slade the contact was prolonged an instant longer than necessary.

"The letter came the day after you left for Los Robles," the girl continued. "My brother was going to take it to you—then we got word you were gone."

As she talked, she regained her composure. The light brown eyes fixed steadily on his. Then they lowered to his chest, her lips curled in a smile, she reached out and lightly touched his ribs.

"But you are very thin, senor—you do not eat well?"

"Not lately," Slade admitted.

"We must feed you well while you are here. We have a very good cook—Lupe. I will tell her to give you big portions, like this—"

She finished with a graceful swirl of her hands, as though outlining a large pile of food. Again her laughing eyes looked boldly into Slade's.

His gaze dropped inadvertently to that tantalizing cleft so inadequately veiled by the thin material of her gown.

With an effort he made himself look again into her eyes—and what he saw in them convinced him that it was not only in physical attributes that Don Ricardo's daughter was mature beyond her years.

"You—you will want to read your letter," Juana Castillo said, her face suddenly serious, her voice soft. "I will not keep you."

When she was gone, Slade closed the door and carried the letter over near the lamp. A glance told him the address was in his sister's ostentatiously elegant hand. He tore the envelope open and took out one small, thin piece of paper covered on both sides with writing in a miniature version of that same hand.

July 21, 1867

Dearest Brother,

I do hope this finds you well—in fact I hope it finds you, out there in that great wide open desert with its wild Indians, wild Mexicans and gold-mad white men. Did you see the latest in Mr. Leslie's Newspaper—but of course you wouldn't see it out there. Yet you are there to see it yourself—I hope.

Oh dear brother how I fear for your safety out in that wild land. How I wish you had not gone—that you were here safe at Shelbourne Farm with me. But of course you did have to go. We must have money—now more than ever—or lose all.

We have had a most miserable time since you left. You remember how the cold hung on so much later than usual—sleet and snow on Easter Day! And the wettest spring in 50 years, all the old folks said—floods—crops washed away.

But all went well—three more foals were dropped after you left. That's five in all, two colts and three fillies—though one of the colts is a puny thing. For that matter, none of them can compare to Warrior King's get. But it was awfully nice of

Mr. Whitlock to let us send the mares you'd picked up from our even-more-destitute neighbors to his Grand Duke. Next year—let's hope Warrior Prince will be here to carry on his sire's line. (And again, dear brother, I fear for you so!)

But I go on so—and must get all this on one small sheet, these postal rates are so awfully high. So to business.

Please write and let me know how your plans progress so I can inform Mr. Marshall. (That is Brent Marshall, who is in sole charge of the bank now, his poor father having passed away last month.)

Mr. Marshall came out to see me last weekend, and asked about you, and how our affairs are going. He is quite concerned that your plans have not gone awry. His father's death has caused problems at the bank, and he is most anxious that we will be able to pay off our note by the 1st of the year. He was also greatly concerned how I was making out in your absence. I had to be frank with him and admit that as much as I have scrimped and saved, I do not see how we can get by much longer here at the Farm. Mr. Marshall, who seems really most kind and understanding, actually offered to let me have a few hundred from his own account to tide us over—though I of course told him I would accept only in the case of the most dire emergency.

Still, you see how desperate things are. Our only hope is for your plans to succeed. So please write me, brother dear, and let me know how things are with you.

I pray for your safety constantly, and live for the

day when my eyes will see you again.
Your most affectionate sister,
                              Nedra

His sister's letter was still on Slade's mind as he sat at the big dining table a little later on with the Castillo family. Though the food was tasty and plentiful, he had little appetite.

When the girl, Juana, chided him playfully—"But Senor Shelbourne, you eat hardly anything—Lupe will think you do not like her cooking"—he gulped down a few mouthfuls. Then the closing phrases of Nedra's letter came to him—"how desperate things are here" and "our only hope is for your plans to succeed"—and he put down his fork.

How was he to succeed with Prince crippled?

A few minutes later men's voices were heard in the patio and Don Jose Sandoval, accompanied by the American banker, Carter Armstrong, entered the room.

Don Jose was tall and slender with a long goatee, something of a Don Juan in appearance, though alert and incisive in manner and speech—which was entirely Spanish.

Carter Armstrong was plumpish and pinkish with slicked-back whitish hair and jovial demeanor more suited to a politician than a banker.

Dona Ysabel and her daughter rose to leave, but on the way out Juana paused beside Slade.

"You seem worried, senor," she said in a low voice. "I hope there was not bad news in your letter."

"No bad news," Slade replied. "Only—well—

business.''

"Business?" The girl's slender eyebrows arched. "The address appeared to be in a woman's hand."

"My sister's, " Slade explained. "She is running our farm in Kentucky."

"Oh, I see."

For an instant her eyes again looked boldly into his, then she said, "You must excuse me, senor, I did not mean to pry into your business," whirled and went through the doorway.

The supper dishes were quickly replaced with cups of strong black coffee and glasses of imported Fundador brandy, cigars were lighted, and as the men sat around the table Slade once more told of the theft of Warrior Prince and its consequences. Though he compressed and edited the account, it was prolonged by the necessity of Carter Armstrong translating for Don Jose.

"So you see," Slade concluded finally, "my horse is lame. He will not be able to race on the date set."

Don Ricardo tapped the ash from his cigar into a copper bowl.

"We wondered if—possibly—Don Jose would agree to postpone the race until Senor Shelbourne's horse recovers."

But the banker, Armstrong, drew a sheaf of papers from an inside pocket of his coat and unfolded them.

"This is the race agreement," he said. "I recall no provision here for a postponement. On the contrary, there is a forfeit clause. If either horse fails to appear on the date set, the stake money goes to the owner of the other horse.''

Armstrong then spoke in Spanish to Don Jose. The thin man responded briefly. The banker turned to Slade.

"Don Jose has obligations. It is very inconvenient for him to keep the stake money tied up much longer. But he does not want to take your money by forfeit. He will agree to postpone the race until your horse recovers."

Armstrong folded the papers, restored them to his pocket.

"I assume this is satisfactory with you, Mr. Shelbourne," he said, starting to rise.

But Slade held up his hand.

"Wait a minute—"

Thoughts that had been sifting through his mind since he first discovered Warrior Prince lame in the corral at Rancho San Lorenzo had suddenly, impelled by the urgency of his sister's letter, evolved into a possible solution to the problem.

Because in spite of Don Jose's generous agreement to a postponement, a problem remained. Realistically, Slade didn't expect Prince to be fit to run for at least three months. That would mean postponing the race until mid-December. The mortgage on Shelbourne Farm was due December 31. He couldn't possibly get the money to Kentucky in time. And according to Nedra's letter, Brent Marshall wouldn't be able to grant even a short extension.

Slade had been searching his brain for an alternative. Now, midst brandy fumes and cigar smoke, it came to him.

"Perhaps," he said, "instead of a delay, Don Jose would agree to a substitute."

"A substitute?" The banker looked startled.

"My mare—Shelbourne Lady. A Thoroughbred, with some of the same blood as the colt. And a runner, though she's never raced because of the war. I don't think she's as fast as the colt, but she's a year older, she might have more stamina in this long a race."

Slade paused to take a swallow of brandy.

"I'll match her against Don Jose's horse for the same stake, on the same conditions."

Armstrong looked doubtful.

"I don't know—these Californians don't think much of mares. They ride only stallions—mares are for women and children. I doubt if Don Jose would run Diablo Negro against a mare."

"Ask him."

Armstrong did. The reply was quick and short—a single word, the same in Spanish as English—

"No."

Slade allowed a lengthy pause to follow that word, then said quietly to Armstrong—

"Ask him if he's afraid my mare will beat his horse."

Armstrong shifted nervously in his chair, cleared his throat, finally spoke in an abjectly apologetic tone.

Don Jose's eyes blazed, red suffused his narrow, normally pallid face. Crackling syllables tumbled from his thin lips.

"Don Jose says," Armstrong translated when the outburst had ended, "that he has no fear your mare will beat Diablo Negro, that he will race his horse against your mare for the same stake, under the same conditions, on the date previously set—September 15th.''

Slade felt a twinge of apprehension.

''What's the date today?''

''September fifth.''

Ten days. Not nearly enough time to bring a horse up to a race, especially a horse that for the last three weeks had been trekking around the Baja California desert on short rations and little water. But a look at Don Jose's sternly set, still flushed face convinced Slade that to ask for another delay —even as little as a week—would be useless.

''All right,'' he said to the banker, ''the fifteenth. Now what do we do, draw up another agreement, or just shake on it—''

Rising from his chair he started to extend his hand toward Don Jose, but the thin man, himself rising quickly, stepped back and spoke a brief phrase in Spanish.

''He says you have his word,'' said Armstrong. ''That will be sufficient.''

''Of course,'' Slade agreed. ''And he has mine.''

After Don Jose and Armstrong had left, Slade turned to Don Ricardo.

''The man who stole my horse—big, blond man. Name's Linc Weaver. Is he back in town?''

Don Ricardo, though he remembered Linc from a month or so before, had not seen him recently.

''But I will ask about him tomorrow,'' he said. ''Possibly he is at one of the ranchos in the country.''

Thinking of Linc reminded Slade of the last time one of his horses had been in a barn of Don Ricardo's—the night Prince was stolen from Rancho Los Robles.

Could he get someone to guard Lady? Someone he could trust?

He thought of Lalo. He should see him anyway, make sure he was all right. The youth had hardly spoken a word during the ride from Rancho San Lorenzo, obviously grieving over the death of his uncle and the loss of his sister.

A little later, having received directions for finding the house of Lalo's aunt, Slade stepped from the doorway and started across the shadowy plaza, dimly lit by oil lamps on the walls of buildings around the square.

He had gone only a few steps when a voice called from behind him.

"Senor."

Turning, he saw two dark shapes outlined against the wall of the Castillo house.

Thinking one of the shapes might be Linc Weaver, Slade dropped his right hand to his hip—and remembered he had left his gunbelt on the bed in his room.

As the shapes approached he realized neither was big enough to be Linc. Had the big man hired someone—a couple of Mexicans—to do his dirty work?

But as the figures drew close he recognized the youth, Lalo.

An instant later he saw who was with him.

It was the boy's sister—Coco.

Chapter 12

Slade's first impulse was to sweep the girl into his arms. But fearing she might misunderstand—after all, he had known her but a few days at the small rancho—he only grasped her hand and smiled down at her.

"Coco! What are you doing here? How did you escape from the Indians?"

"So many questions!" The girl drew back in mock alarm, then looked around. "And this is no place to talk." As she pulled a dark rebozo closer around her shoulders Slade realized a damp chill had come into the night air.

"Come," Coco said, "let's go to my aunt's house, I'll make us some chocolate and tell you all that happened."

The aunt's house, close to the river bed, was very small, and the aunt was very fat, but with the four of them squeezed around a tiny table over steaming cups of frothy chocolate, Coco told her story.

"I didn't escape from the Indians—because the Indians never got me. Another of the sons of the Garcias, the people who came to stay with me"— she paused to cross herself—"came down that morning from their rancho. A boy called Timas. He was going to the coast to catch fish, which he meant to bring back to the rancho and dry. I went with him to help carry the fish back. When we got home that evening we found the Indians had been there"—she choked back a sob—"and the others were dead."

Coco paused again, wiped a tear from her cheek, took a sip of chocolate.

"We saw the Indians had gone east, so we went back to the coast. We knew we could get food there—crabs, fish—the Indians had taken everything from the rancho."

"Not quite everything," Slade put in, and he told her of the pot of beans he and Lalo had found in the wreckage.

"I wish we'd found them," said Coco. "I got very tired of fish by the time we got to San Diego."

"You stayed on the coast all the way?" Slade asked.

The girl nodded.

"Why didn't you go to one of the other ranchos —like San Lorenzo?"

"We were afraid. We thought the Indians might double back and attack another rancho. So we stayed close to the sea until we got to San Diego."

They had finally reached the town only two days before, footsore and half-starved—but safe.

"Gracias a dios," the girl concluded, crossing herself again.

"Amen," said Slade. Impulsively, his hand went out to cover hers where it lay on the table. Her soft eyes smiled into his. But moments later they misted over as he said, with a nod toward her brother—

"Lalo has told you about Tio Luis?"

Coco nodded. "He was like a father to us," she

said, a tremor again in her voice.

"He was a very fine man," Slade said.

The girl nodded again. Her lower lip trembled momentarily, then she shook herself, squared her shoulders, stood up—

"More chocolate, senor?" she asked, reaching for his cup.

But Slade declined. Rather than disturb this reunion of sister and brother, he decided to stand watch over Lady himself tonight. He asked Lalo to come in the morning to help him care for the mare.

Back at the Castillo house he got his blankets and went out to the barn. He made himself a bed of hay on the hardpacked dirt in front of Lady's stall, took off his boots and hat and wrapped himself in the blankets.

At the first faint gray of dawn he rolled up his blankets, saddled Lady and rode out of town. Rounding the point of the hill, he set her at an easy gallop along the sandy road that led east up the broad, flat river valley. They had covered about three miles, and he could make out the crumbling facade of the old mission on a rise about the same distance ahead, when the sun appeared above the low hills beyond.

Pulling Lady up, he headed her back toward town, again at a moderate gallop.

The sun was growing warm on his back as they rounded the end of the low hills that skirted the bay, but the town lay in the shadow of the brush-covered hillside, on which a few mounds of dirt and rocks were all that remained of the original Spanish presidio. Wisps of smoke spiraled lazily up through haze-laden air redolent of burning mesquite roots, hot grease, bacon and beans, coffee and chocolate. Here and there people moved around—a boy leading a skinny cow in for milking, a man walking quickly down a well-worn path to an outhouse, a woman plucking tomatoes from a vine sprawling across most of the backyard of a small plank-siding house. Somewhere a dog yapped, a burro vented his frustration in a long, hiccuping bray.

Outside the Castillo barn Slade unsaddled Lady, washed her and rubbed her down.

"Buenos dias senor."

Turning, he found Juana Castillo watching him from the patio gate. Hair pulled tightly back in two braids and the snug fit of a dark skirt around a trim waist gave her even more of a little-girl look this morning—belied by the swelling outlines under her blouse.

"Buenos dias senorita, como esta usted?" Slade said, and the Spanish response earned him a warm smile and a "Muy bien, gracias."

Then switching to English—

"You are up very early, senor."

"It's the best time to work a horse," Slade explained. "Before they've eaten—before the heat of the day."

"Your mare is very beautiful," Juana said, and moving quickly forward she ran a hand along Lady's still-damp neck. "But do you really think she can beat Diablo Negro?"

"I think so. I wish there was more time to train her for the race. But I think she can win anyway."

The girl looked doubtful.

"Diablo Negro is very fast—very strong. He has won many races—no horse in California has ever been close to him. He has the finest blood from Spain—"

Slade reached up and straightened the mare's forelock.

"Lady has the finest blood of England, Virginia and Kentucky—she's fast and strong."

"But the race will be very long—to the end of Point Loma and back. I think almost four leguas. Won't that favor the horse over the mare?"

"Back home before the war Lady's sire and dam ran races in four mile heats—sometimes three heats. That's 12 miles—I think about the same as your four leguas."

The girl remained unconvinced.

"I still think Diablo Negro will win. I will make you a bet, senor."

"All right," Slade responded quickly. "What do you want to bet?"

She looked up at him through long, soft eyelashes.

"Cualquier te gustas, senor."

Slade gulped. "Whatever you like." And she had used the familiar "te gustas." Did she mean—?

The bold, challenging gaze of those light brown eyes told him Juana Castillo meant exactly that. But there must be a catch to it.

"Against what?"

"Cualquier me gusta."

Whatever she liked!

"It's a bet," he said, his voice suddenly hoarse, and looked deep into those eyes for another long moment before they were interrupted by the arrival of Lalo, come to help with Lady.

Telling the youth to walk Lady about half an hour, then give her hay and grain, Slade strolled with Juana through the peaceful, flower-scented patio and into the house for breakfast.

Nine days later, the day of the race, the patio was anything but peaceful—in fact was a bustle of activity—as Slade hurried across it from the barn at almost the same early hour.

The activity involved a horde of Indian servants preparing for the big fandango Don Ricardo was giving in celebration of the race.

But the fandango—even the race itself—had been pushed into the background of Slade's thoughts by the events of the past few hours.

There had been a smaller, private baile at the Castillo house the night before, limited to close friends and family, including a host of cousins. Juana Castillo was constantly introducing people to Slade as "mi primo Manuel" or "mi prima Carmen."

Slade, excusing himself shortly before midnight to go out to the barn and check on Lady, had been surprised to find, in the flickering light of an oil lamp, Lalo, wrapped in a sarape, propped against the wall opposite the mare's stall.

"What the hell are you doing here?" Slade asked. "I told you to go home and get a good night's sleep. If you're going to ride that race tomorrow—"

It was a decision he had made only that morning.

He had fully intended to ride the race himself. But a few days before, afflicted by a sudden attack of cramps and diarrhea, he had allowed Lalo to gallop Lady while he watched from a vantage point conveniently near a clump of brush. The youth had done well, and though Slade felt better the next day, he let Lalo work the mare again—and started thinking seriously of having him ride the race.

The reason, of course, was weight. Lalo was at least forty pounds lighter than Slade. Forty pounds would be a tremendous factor in a twelve-mile race. On the other hand—the other side of the scale, Slade thought wryly—there was his own knowledge of racing, of racehorses, of Lady in particular.

Then someone pointed out Don Jose's rider passing through the plaza on Diablo Negro. He was a wizened little Indian of barely a hundred pounds.

The next morning Slade mounted one of Don Ricardo's horses, Lalo riding Lady, and they went slowly over the course—westward along the beach road, skirting mudflats for about three miles, up a winding canyon and along the crest of the long isthmus to the lighthouse at its tip. As they rode, Slade discussed race strategy and the condition of the course. Where to ease Lady over sandy surface; where to stay off the road, deeply rutted by cart traffic, entirely.

The morning of the day before the race, meeting with Don Ricardo, Don Jose and Carter Armstrong to discuss final arrangements, Slade formally named Lalo Gonzalez to ride Lady.

So what was the youth doing in the barn the night before, after Slade had arranged for one of Don Ricardo's most trusted vaqueros to watch over Lady?

"I couldn't sleep at home, senor," Lalo replied to his question. "I think too much about the race. So I come here, to guard Lady." He held up Tio Luis's old octagon-barreled muzzle loader.

"No one will harm her, senor."

"All right," Slade gave in grudgingly. "Just be sure you don't fall asleep."

Not much danger of that, Slade decided a couple of hours later as he lay awake himself in the brass bed, staring at the ceiling. Between the sounds of voices and music from the still-continuing baile in the patio, and his anxiety about the race—

The race he had to win.

Worries chased through his head, preventing sleep. Worries about Lady's condition. She seemed fit enough, but there had been so little time. About Lalo. He rode well—but he had no experience. Don Jose's Indian rider was a veteran of many races. Would Lalo be able to judge the pace? If it was too fast, would the mare be able to match the stallion's greater size and strength at the finish? If it was too slow, would the wily Indian rider be able to get a final burst of speed out of his mount and catch Lalo by surprise in the last strides?

It would be best, Slade decided, to instruct Lalo to let the mare choose her own pace.

Another worry loomed larger in his mind—where was Linc Weaver? Though all inquiries about the big blond man had brought negative replies, Slade couldn't entirely banish the fear that he was lurking somewhere, waiting to strike one last, disastrous blow.

The baile finally broke up. After a series of "Hasta mananas"—a misuse of the expression, Slade reflected, it must be almost 3 a.m.—the house became silent. Still he lay awake, staring at the ceiling, the corner of his eye catching a faint flicker of light reflected off one of the brass posts at the foot of the bed.

He must have finally dozed off, because suddenly he found himself sitting straight up in bed, cold sweat coating his body.

Had he heard someone cry out? Or was it the remnant of a dream?

Whichever, he had an overpowering feeling something was wrong.

He jumped out of bed, hauled on his trousers and hurried, barefoot and bare-chested, across the patio.

The entrance to the barn loomed dark and forbidding. What had happened to the lamp? To Lalo?

Slade paused in the doorway, regretting the haste that had brought him here without the Colt—without a weapon of any kind.

Straining his eyes in a vain attempt to penetrate the black interior, he took a cautious step forward —another—

Hearing a faint sound, sensing movement, he turned toward Lady's stall, crouched—

The instinctive bending of the knees, the forward

lean of the body, saved him. Something hard—a gun barrel?—instead of smashing his skull at the temple merely grazed his head.

He stepped forward, swung blindly. His fist dug deep into a paunchy belly. His uppercut glanced off the hard angle of a jaw, brought a muffled grunt.

Then powerful arms were around him, lifting him off his feet, throwing him backwards, staggering, smashing against the wall.

He bounced off, swung, hit bone that crunched beneath his fist and sent stinging pain from knuckles up through elbow to his shoulder. Dug his other fist deep into that paunch again, then swung for the head but missed—

And was caught in those bear-strong arms again —carried back—smashed against the 'dobe wall with a crash that went off like a bomb in his head.

Felt himself whirling down toward limitless space—with his last strength threw back his head and yelled—a hoarse, strangled, wordless shout. Yelled again, heard faintly the sound of receding footsteps before darkness closed in completely.

Sensation returned slowly, starting with a dully throbbing pain at the back of his head. He got his hand back there, it came away wet. As strength seeped back into his body he got to his knees, finally was standing, swaying, wiping more wetness from his face, out of his eyes.

Hazily aware that the first hint of day was lightening the inside of the barn, he stumbled to Lady's stall; found the mare there, apparently unharmed.

On the other side of the barn he knelt beside Lalo's motionless form, looked down at the youth's battered and bloodied features, saw a frothy pink bubble appear between smashed lips, a bubble that grew and burst. Felt for and found a faint pulse alongside his throat. Lalo was alive—barely.

Slade left him in the barn and went to the house to get help. A doctor arrived in a few minutes. After a lengthy examination the youth was moved on an improvised rawhide stretcher to the house—in fact to the brass bed in Slade's room.

While the doctor worked on Lalo, outside in the patio an old Indian woman, evidently a longtime servant of the Castillos, tended to Slade's head wounds. She cut away the blood-matted hair where the back of his head had smashed against the wall, washed the scraped flesh with a foul-smelling, sharply astringent solution, and applied the same treatment to the cut just above his hairline in front.

When she had finished, Slade hurried back to the barn.

Finding Lady unharmed, he saddled her, mounted, headed for the valley road and gave her a brisk half-mile race day blowout.

Though the exertion left his head throbbing, he walked the mare back to the barn, rubbed her down, gave her water, hay, and a half-measure of grain. Then he hurried to the house.

His light rap at the door to his room was answered quickly by Coco, who, after a glance over her shoulder, stepped outside and quietly closed the door.

"How is he?" Slade asked.

"The doctor thinks he will be all right."

"Is he conscious? Can he talk? Does he know who did it?"

The girl shook her head.

"He woke up, but he could talk only a little. He remembers that the light went out—someone hit him. He doesn't know who."

Slade hadn't really expected the youth would be able to identify his attacker. But from the size and strength of the man he'd fought with in the dark, he felt certain it was Linc Weaver.

"I'm sorry, Senor Slade," Coco continued with an apologetic smile, "I don't think Lalo can ride for you in the race today."

It was better this way, Slade thought when, a little before five o'clock, he led Lady from the barn down the street between the Castillo and Sandoval houses and into the plaza. Better that he ride the mare, in spite of the weight handicap. Then he could make the decisions as to pace. He could tell how the mare was handling the going—whether she would be able to last the distance. And if not, if she showed signs of distress, or met with an accident —stepped in a hole—stumbled badly—he would pull up. Even if it meant losing the race—meant losing Shelbourne Farm—he would pull up rather than risk permanent injury—perhaps death—for his horse.

The plaza, that normally near-deserted dusty rectangle decorated only by a rickety flagpole and an old Spanish cannon, had come alive this afternoon. It was so crowded that Slade had to pick his way carefully through the throng toward the make-shift officials' stand that had been knocked together from rough lumber in front of the shack that served as a town hall.

There were people of all ages, from toddling tots to hobbling ancients, ranging in complexion from powder white through red-mahogany to ebony, in costume from the gold-and-silver-decorated finery of the resplendent Dons to the multi-patched rags of indigent Indians.

The crowd was about ninety-five per cent male, the remainder mostly Indian women with stumpy bodies and sagging old-before-their-time faces. Perhaps half the men were Californios, another third anglo-American, the rest Indians.

Of the Californios, almost all were mounted, most were at least half drunk. Of the Indians, all were on foot, all were drunk. Of the Americans, only a few were mounted, and to Slade it seemed that only he was wholly sober.

While there were few women in the plaza, many could be seen gazing from the iron-barred windows of surrounding houses. And the cupola on top of the Castillo house was a rainbow of colored fabrics as Dona Ysabel, Juana, and a covey of feminine friends clustered there. More bright gowns, cut to expose powdered shoulders and copious cleavage, adorned the ample figures of a number of women draped over the railing of the third-floor balcony of the Franklin Hotel.

In front of the Franklin the crowd milled thickest, and from inside the hubbub was punctuated by scraping fiddles, stamping feet and frequent shouts. From a cantina across the plaza blaring trumpets and thrumming guitars accompanied voices shrilling ranchero songs.

As Slade led Lady toward the officials' stand the mare reacted to the excitement of the crowd, flinging her head high, flaring her nostrils, lifting her hoofs as she pranced in time with the music.

When they reached the stand—an unrailed platform about six-by-six, no more than three feet high with a packing box to serve as a step—Slade soothed the mare by stroking her glistening neck and talking to her softly.

Though it could be no more than a few minutes before five, no officials were around.

Slade kept a sharp eye on the surrounding throng. In particular he watched for a big man with light hair. He was convinced that, for whatever mysterious reason, Linc was still trying to prevent him from winning this race. He felt certain Linc had tried again early that morning—and failed again.

Would he make one more desperate attempt?

It was a long race, and over most of the course the racers would be out of sight of spectators. A party of men had ridden out earlier to the lighthouse to make sure both contestants rounded that most distant point on the course. But between the town and the lighthouse anyone planning skulduggery would have little to fear of witnesses.

With that in mind, Slade had been tempted, after donning a jersey striped red and blue—Shelbourne Farm's racing colors—to strap his gunbelt around his waist. But the Navy Colt, though lighter than Army and Dragoon models, still weighed upwards of five pounds—and Lady was already conceding about fifty to Don Jose's horse. So Slade contented himself with the holstered Bowie knife on his belt—and now watched the crowd. If he could spot Linc—

But when he did recognize a face in the crowd, it wasn't Linc Weaver. It was the slender, handsome ranchero from Rancho San Lorenzo, Roberto Rodriguez.

"Ola, amigo!" cried Rodriguez, grasping Slade's hand. "I came to see the race—and"—he winked—"to win some dinero on your mare."

"I hope you do," said Slade. "But how is Prince?"

"Your colt is much better. I think in two or three weeks we can bring him to San Diego."

"That may be in time for this race," Slade remarked wryly, looking around. Though it was now after five, there was still no sign of race officials—or the competition.

Rodriguez shrugged. "We Californios have a saying—'Tiempo no importa.' Time doesn't matter."

Slade glanced toward the descending sun.

"If we're going to get this race in before dark, time damn well better matter."

But a few minutes later Don Ricardo Castillo and Carter Armstrong arrived and took their placed on the officials' stand. Not long after that there was a stir in the crowd and from the direction of the Sandoval house at the far corner of the plaza Don Jose's big black stallion appeared. Perched on his back, bare to the waist, was his diminutive Indian rider.

When they drew close, Slade saw the Indian was using a conventional California saddle—hide over a wood frame. Lady's lightweight English racing saddle would compensate for some of the weight difference.

Even after Diablo Negro and his rider reached the officials' stand there was considerable delay. First Carter Armstrong carefully went over the conditions. Then two rows of men were posted, with reatas strung between them to keep the crowd back until the racers had left the plaza.

Slade delayed mounting until this had been accomplished—another slight advantage for Lady, as the Indian had remained astride Diablo Negro. It wasn't until Armstrong called the contestants to the starting point that he tightened Lady's girth and swung into the saddle.

For a few seconds the mare and the stallion danced nervously, side by side—then Don Ricardo raised his pistol and with a puff of smoke and a sharp "Crack!" the race was on.

Chapter 13

The black stallion and the dark chestnut mare lunged forward as one. Hoofs thundering on hard-packed dirt, they charged down the corridor through the tight-packed, cheering crowd, sped on by shouts of "Vaya Diablo!" and "Go Yank!"

Leaving the plaza they swung left onto the beach road, pounding across the sandy delta of the now dry river, which over centuries had shifted its course countless times. Sometimes it emptied into the main bay south of the point, sometimes into what was called False Bay to the north. To the south lay tidal mudflats, the stench from which was normally carried away from town by the prevailing northwest breeze.

For half a mile stallion and mare went head-to-head, shoulder-to-shoulder. Slade saw quickly they were very evenly matched in speed. But speed alone wouldn't decide this race. Over the 12-mile course, stamina would be the critical factor.

As the road swung right, skirting the mudflats, Slade began to take Lady in hand. Briefly the mare resisted.

"Easy, girl, easy," he called, tightening his pull on the reins. "Long way to go—let's take our time."

Grudgingly Lady acknowledged his command, settled into a ground-devouring gait she could keep up almost indefinitely.

Diablo Negro's rider also sought to slow his mount. But competitive fire blazed in the stallion's blood. Tossing his head, arching his neck, he fought against the heavy Spanish bit. They had gone another quarter of a mile before the Indian got him under control.

By this time the black had pulled out to a lead of about 10 lengths. Slade eased his hold slightly, until Lady had cut that margin in half. Then he held her there, far enough back to avoid clods and rocks flying up from the stallion's hoofs, but close enough to make him constantly aware they were dogging him, keeping the pressure on.

They continued at this steady pace while a mile went by, and another.

Then the road, which had been skirting the slowly rising bulk of the peninsula, forked. The left fork followed the shoreline to the settlement of La Playa, where occasional ships still anchored in the lee of Ballast Point and whalers' trying vats were spotted among remnants of hide houses recalling the boom years of the leather trade.

But the race course followed the right fork, a steeper, rougher road that climbed a canyon onto the broad spine of the peninsula.

At first this canyon, occasionally cut by smaller side canyons, ran due north. Then, at a point Slade judged to be midway out the peninsula, one quarter of the full distance of the race, the canyon swung west. The road became narrower and steeper. The black was forced to slow his pace, and the gap narrowed until Lady was only a couple of lengths from the stallion's heavily muscled hindquarters.

Diablo's rider looked back, saw how close they were. He leaned forward and gave a shrill yell in his mount's ear, simultaneously lashing his flank with the loose ends of the reins.

Lunging forward, the stallion took a misstep, bobbled, almost went down.

His rider, caught unaware, was flung forward.

As Lady ranged up alongside the still stumbling Diablo, Slade saw the Indian make a frantic grab at the black's flying mane, catch it for an instant, then lose his grip and plunge over the stallion's shoulder.

Lady shied away from the falling rider and for a few seconds Slade had his own hands full. When he was able to look back he saw the Indian on the ground, hanging desperately onto the end of one rein. The black had dragged him some distance, but was now halted, head low, neck bowed, fighting to get free.

For a moment Slade felt the instinctive horseman's reaction to go back and help. Then he remembered the money at stake—and the fact that Lady was already doubly handicapped; by his weight compared to the tiny Indian's, and by the lingering effects of the Baja ordeal.

He turned his attention ahead. The road still rose slightly between low hills. It ran through dry grassland, with only occasional clumps of brush and here and there some scrub oak. The sun, low over the rugged headland, glared into his eyes.

Looking back again, Slade saw that the Indian was on his feet, trying to remount, but getting no cooperation from the lunging, plunging stallion. Until finally the rider slashed the black savagely around the head with the loose ends of the reins, forcing him to stand still for an instant—leaped on his back, gathered the reins and turned him, sent him charging along in pursuit.

But by this time Slade and Lady were far in the lead, galloping over gently rolling ground, the ocean now visible on each side of the steadily narrowing peninsula.

Up ahead, on a knoll surmounting the headland, Slade saw the boxy, two-chimneyed shape of the gray brick lighthouse. Rays of the lower sun glinted off glass enclosing the lantern atop the squatty, iron-railing-girdled tower, as though the light was beckoning them to this midpoint of the race.

As they drew closer, Slade could make out several men and horses grouped at the near corner of the white picket fence separating the lighthouse from its barren, windswept surroundings. These would be the judges; two Americans and two Californios, and the lighthouse keeper and his assistant. On a platform adjoining the wooden shed attached to the north side of the building, several women and children stood—the keepers' families.

As Lady galloped strongly up the final slope, the women waved, men and children cheered—all except the two Californios, who stared glumly off at the distant Diablo Negro.

A shout of "Keep it up Yank!" echoed in Slade's ears as, having guided Lady around the lighthouse, he headed her back down the road.

Diablo Negro was approaching. As the distance between them quickly narrowed, Slade saw that the stallion's rider had been driving him hard to catch up. The black coat was glossy with sweat, foam-streaked where neck joined shoulders. Distended blood-pink nostrils sucked in air.

But the Indian yelled and lashed the stallion with the reins as they went by.

Lady, without urging, continued strongly and easily along the road curving among the broad, rolling contours atop the peninsula. At the base of the distant hills Slade could just make out the buildings of San Diego, their 'dobe walls gilded by the setting sun.

It was all downhill from here.

But he deliberately suppressed a surge of confidence. Certainly they appeared to have the race won. But there was more than a quarter of the distance—better than three miles—still to go.

He glanced over his shoulder as they began the descent into the canyon. Diablo Negro was still far behind. He slowed Lady, keeping a sharp eye on the sometimes deeply rutted and rock-strewn road. At this point, haste could lose the race. If Lady took a misstep, injured herself—

As they dropped lower, the hills behind cut off the sun. When the canyon angled south toward the bay, the steep slope on their right cast a pall of twilight gloom over the road. Sparks flew as Lady's steel-shod hoofs struck rock.

Straining his eyes to spot hazards in the road, Slade didn't notice the rider partly screened by high brush alongside the trail until they were almost upon him.

When he did see him—the upraised arm—leveled pistol—he knew instantly there was but one thing to do.

Hauling Lady's head over, booting heels into her ribs, leaning over her neck, he sent the mare in a crashing leap through the brush, straight at the other horseman—

Flame flared from the revolver's muzzle, white-hot fire seared Slade's side, then Lady smashed full speed into the other horse, knocking it sideways—back on its haunches—falling—throwing its rider clear—

And as that rider crashed to the ground with an impact that jolted the gun from his hand, Slade launched himself from the saddle and smashed down on top of a stupefied Linc Weaver—a Linc Weaver with dyed dark hair betrayed by yellow stubble coating his jaw.

As awareness returned to Linc's face, as the heavy body tensed, Slade snatched the Bowie knife from its scabbard and laid its keen edge across Linc's throat, speaking the first words that came to his mind.

"Why—Linc—why?"

And remembered another time he had held a knife to Linc's throat—asked that same question—in a tunnel beneath the Ohio State Penitentiary. And the long-delayed unsatisfactory answer.

This time the answer came immediately.

"For money—what else?" Linc growled. Then, hate blazing from those pale blue eyes—

"But you wouldn't know about that—you with yore rich folks—yore fancy farm—you a high-n-mighty officer with yore pretty unyform and yore fast-steppin' horses—"

So that was it. Linc Weaver, reared in poverty on a rocky Cumberland farm, saw Slade as a symbol of Bluegrass wealth.

If he only knew!

No time to go into that now. But there was another question.

"Whose money, Linc?"

Defiance blazed from Linc's eyes.

"You'd like to know, wouldn't you?"

Slade increased the pressure of the Bowie on Linc's throat. A thin line of blood appeared. He raised the knife, held the crimson-edged blade before Linc's eyes.

"Whose money, Linc?"

"Carter Armstrong's."

"The banker? How much? Why?"

"A thousand. So you lose—he can keep yore stake."

"But Don Jose would get my stake."

"Don Jose owes Armstrong twenty thousand dollars, at high interest. Has no cash. Armstrong put up his stake. Paid me five-hundred-threw in that treasure map—to steal yore colt so you'd have to default. When you fixed it to run the mare instead, he promised me five-hundred more to make you lose."

Slade returned the Bowie to Linc's throat, bore

down a hair harder—

"Proof, Linc. Can you give me proof?"

"Shore. Got it in writin'."

"Where?"

"Shirt pocket."

Still holding the knife against Linc's throat, Slade reached into his pocket, took out a wrinkled piece of paper, held it up to read in the dim light—

Suddenly Linc's body heaved under him. A big fist struck his wrist, knocking it away from Linc's throat, sending the Bowie flying off into the brush. The big man's other fist smashed into his face—

Stunned, Slade felt those muscular arms around him, pulling him down, Linc rolling on top. Felt Linc's bearlike grip—the same chest-crushing force he'd felt that morning in the Castillo barn.

Squirming, struggling, he fought to break free—without success. His right hand, groping, closed on something round and hard—a good-sized rock. If he could only—

But Linc's mighty strength held him powerless, arms pinned helplessly at his sides. His face was buried in the big man's shoulder—he was smothering—

Desperate for air, he forced his jaws open—and then with sudden inspiration closed them again savagely on Linc Weaver's flesh.

The big man howled. For an instant his grip slackened—just long enough for Slade to jerk his right arm free, swing his hand, tightly gripping the rock, with all his force against the side of Linc's head—

The muscles of those powerful arms contracted

again—crushing him. For what seemed minutes but could only have been split seconds the breath-stifling pressure continued—then Linc's body suddenly relaxed—slumped.

Slade rolled the hulk off him, rose, leaned over the big man. His eyes were closed, but he was breathing. A place on the side of his head was growing dark—swelling—

Slade straightened, sucking air into his own lungs. Blood drummed in his ears.

He heard another drumming sound. The drumming of a horse's hoofs pounding on the road.

He looked around just in time to see a dark form rush past, hear the Indian's triumphant shout—

Diablo Negro!

Lady was standing a few yards away. Slade ran to her, grabbed the reins, leaped into the saddle—sent her galloping off in pursuit of the black stallion.

Chapter 14

Out of the canyon, down on the flat road skirting the mudflats, Slade saw that the situation was reversed. Now it was Don Jose's horse that was far ahead.

But with a difference. Now there was less than three miles to go. Could Lady possibly catch the stallion in that distance?

Fortunately, she seemed to have suffered no ill effects from the collision with Linc's horse. But there was the weight factor. And condition.

Slade became aware his left hand still clutched the paper he'd taken from Linc's pocket. He wondered what it said. But there was no time to read it now. He stuffed it in his pocket.

Leaning far forward, he turned his body to the rhythm of the mare as she bounded over the road in the hoofprints of the black horse. Yet, anxious as he was to make up ground, he resisted the impulse to urge Lady all out. He'd seen too many races lost by riders who made their move too soon.

Yards became furlongs, and furlongs became a mile. They were gaining, but with agonizing slowness. As they inched closer to the stallion, the buildings of the town seemed to fly toward them.

Still he kept Lady under light restraint.

Another mile, and they were considerably closer. Was Diablo Negro tiring? As they approached the riverbed the stallion's stride appeared to be shortening, becoming choppy.

But as Lady's hoofs thudded on the softer, sandier going, Slade sensed that she, too, was weakening.

Still she gained—closing the gap with every stride. Until, as they passed the houses on the outskirts of town, the black's lead had shrunk to half a dozen lengths.

Then they were making the turn into the plaza—Diablo Negro swinging wide—Slade guiding Lady through on the inside—saving ground—and suddenly the margin was less than a length.

Thundering down the short lane, through the wildly cheering crowd, again held back by reatas, the mare thrust her nose up even with the stallion's rider, who was slashing his mount at every stride with those long rein ends.

Still Lady moved up—her head at Diablo Negro's chest—his throatlach—

And there she hung.

Slade felt the mare faltering, leaned far forward —tried to lift her with the reins—yelled at her flat-back ears—"Get 'im girl—get 'im!"

And from deep inside her—from generations of Thoroughbred breeding—from her Arab progenitors—Shelbourne Lady summoned something extra.

She drove up head-and-head with the stallion—nose-and-nose—and just yards from the finish she drew ahead.

More than two blocks down the road, beyond the red brick Whaley house, Slade got her pulled up, let her stand a moment, then sent her cantering back toward the finish. At the edge of the plaza he had to rein her to a walk as the crowd gathered around them.

Only a little beyond the finish they came to Diablo Negro. Don Jose's strapping stallion stood, head hanging, spraddle-legged, covered with foam, his sides heaving, whole body trembling with exhaustion. His rider had dismounted.

Lady, by contrast, though sweaty and foam-flecked on neck and shoulders, walked confidently toward the officials' stand, head high, looking out over the crowd.

Through clouds of dust turned gold by the setting sun, Slade saw Don Ricardo Castillo, with agility belying his bulk, drop down from the offi-cials' stand and stride toward him, hand out-stretched.

"Felicidades, senor. You have won a great race. Your mare was magnificent."

Slade shook his hand, said "Thank you," dismounted. Finding his legs a little unsteady, he clutched the saddle for a moment. As he lowered his arms, a pain in his side recalled the flash of Linc's pistol—the burning sensation.

Looking down, he saw a damp stain on his jersey. Raising it, he found a red furrow just inches below his ribcage.

"You are hurt, senor," said Don Ricardo. "What happened?"

"A little trouble out there." Slade nodded

toward the peninsula. "No problem."

Don Ricardo eyed him questioningly, but when Slade volunteered no further explanation, his heavy shoulders moved in a massive shrug.

"We must have your wound cared for," he said. "Then we will meet with Don Jose and Senor Armstrong to settle the wager."

"That can wait," said Slade. "I've got to take care of my mare first."

But before leading Lady away he looked toward the officials' stand where Carter Armstrong still stood.

Could it wait? he wondered, thinking of what Linc had revealed.

It would have to.

An hour later, having cooled out Lady and rubbed her down, and had the bullet scrape on his side tended to by the same old woman who had ministered to his injuries that morning, Slade entered Don Ricardo's study, a small room off the main sala.

From outside, the whoops and hollers of a combined post-race celebration and burgeoning fandango penetrated the thick 'dobe walls of the Castillo house. But in the small room three solemn men, seated at a round mahogany table, awaited Slade.

Don Ricardo rose as he entered, pulled out a chair for him, took a bottle of Fundador from a sideboard and poured a generous amount into a glass—topped off his own glass and those in front of Don Jose Sandoval and Carter Armstrong.

"Al ganador," he toasted, raising his glass.

"To the winner," murmured Carter Armstrong. Was it Slade's imagination, or was there a hint of mockery in his voice?

"To Shelbourne Lady," Slade responded, and he let two large swallows of the fruity brandy slide down his throat. Sitting down, he let his hand rest on his thigh, comfortably near the Navy Colt once again holstered on his hip.

A long silence followed Slade's counter-toast, broken only by muffled sounds of outside merry-making. Slade let his eyes drift from face to face of the other three men.

Don Ricardo's beefy countenance was sullenly embarrassed. After resuming his seat he met Slade's glance only momentarily, then lowered his eyes to the table.

Don Jose, stroking his goatee, stared back at him with aristocratic pride and defiance.

Carter Armstrong's suave countenance reflected the confidence of a poker player with a pat hand.

Slade waited. He had a strong feeling whoever broke this silence would be at a disadvantage.

The first sound came from Don Ricardo. He cleared his throat and looked pointedly at Carter Armstrong.

The banker straightened in his chair.

"Let's get down to business, gentlemen."

From the floor beside his chair he lifted a heavy object, placed it on the table. Slade recognized the canvas moneybelt he had brought—in a specially made saddlebag for it was too heavy to wear—from Kentucky. In each of one-hundred individual pockets of the belt was sewn a fifty-dollar gold piece. Five thousand dollars in all, his stake money.

Slade waited, still silent. Where was Don Jose's money?

"Mr. Shelbourne," the banker said after another lengthy pause, "we have a problem—a very embarrassing situation—"

Slade eyed him levelly.

"Yes, Mr. Armstrong?"

"Well, you see—the money Don Jose put up for the race—it was borrowed from the bank. Don Jose has borrowed, in recent years, a great deal of money from the bank. Now this additional sum—with interest—well—"

The banker leaned back in his chair, hooked his thumbs in small pockets of his vest, and spread pudgy fingers over his gold-watch-chain-girdled paunch.

"Under the circumstances," he resumed in unctuous tones, "I must exercise the bank's prior claim to that money."

Slade tossed off the rest of his brandy, set the glass down firmly. From his pocket he pulled the paper he'd taken from Linc Weaver, placed it on the tabletop and smoothed out the creases. Finally he began to read—

"The undersigned promises to pay Linc Weaver the sum of five-hundred dollars for preventing a horse owned by—"

"Wait!"

Slade looked at Carter Armstrong. The banker's pink face had faded to pasty white, sweat beaded his forehead.

"Where did you get—I mean that paper is obviously a forgery."

He turned to Don Ricardo and Don Jose.

"Surely you gentlemen don't believe that I would—"

"Who said anything about you?" Slade broke in. "Did I say this paper involved you?"

Now he addressed the two Californios.

"Senores, I will tell you now that this paper—which promises to pay Linc Weaver five hundred dollars to keep my horse from winning today's race—is indeed signed by Mr. Armstrong. And his own words just now prove it is no forgery. Here—see for yourself. I'm sure you gentlemen are familiar with Mr. Armstrong's signature."

He tossed the paper over to Don Ricardo. While the two Californios examined it, Slade continued—

"More than that, Linc Weaver told me Armstrong previously paid him to steal my colt, Warrior Prince, so I wuld have to default on the original race agreement."

Don Jose murmured something in Spanish to Don Ricardo, who nodded his head and turned to Armstrong.

"It looks like your signature," he said. "This is a very serious matter, Senor Armstrong. San Diego is a small town, but we are now part of the state of California. We have laws—and judges—"

"It's my word against his," the banker blustered, his face now passing back through pink to fiery red.

"Mine," Slade broke in, "and Linc Weaver's."

He said it knowing the words were pure bluff.

He wasn't even sure Linc was still alive—he'd hit him pretty hard with that rock. If he was alive, it wasn't likely he'd linger long in the vicinity of San Diego.

Pure bluff—but Armstrong fell for it. As Slade's eyes bored into his the banker's gaze dropped, he cleared his throat, pushed back his chair and stood up—

"All right—all right. I'll go get the money."

Slade, too, rose, letting his hand rest on the butt of the Colt.

"Why don't we all go?"

Half an hour later, his own money belt and a good-sized chamois bag containing an equal amount in gold coinage stowed away in Don Ricardo's private safe, Slade stepped into the big sala—living room—of the Castillo residence.

Many heavy pieces of furniture—tables and couches—had been removed, the rest pushed back against the walls; rugs were rolled up leaving bare tile floors cleared for dancing. In one corner black-suited musicians with violins and guitars prepared to play.

"Oh, Senor Shelbourne—there you are!"

It was a moment before Slade recognized the girl hurrying toward him as Juana Castillo. Her light hair was elaborately swirled and coifed high on a tortoise-shell Spanish comb from which descended a mantilla of finest white lace. Her gown was pearl-white, shiny silk and stiff brocade ornamented with beaded designs in gleaming silver, cut to leave golden shoulders bare and give breathtaking glimpses of creamy swelling breasts.

"Congratulations," she said, standing very close to him, looking up into his face. "Your mare was wonderful! What an exciting race! What a thrilling finish! Maravilloso!"

Long lashes veiled her eyes for a moment.

"But I have lost my bet—I must pay you—"

A faint flush appeared on the golden cheeks, but there was no embarrassment in the brown eyes looking into his—in fact, quite the opposite.

Slade felt his own face grow warm.

"There's no hurry about that—senorita."

Still her eyes looked into his—when she spoke, it was barely a whisper.

"There will be a time—and a place—senor."

Then she tossed her head.

"But I am forgetting—"

Turning slightly away, she plucked something from the bodice of her gown, held it out to him.

"This arrived today—I couldn't get it to you earlier."

Their fingers touched as he took a letter, still warm and—though it could have been his imagination—bearing a slight scent of her body.

Again he recognized the elaborate penmanship of his sister.

"If you'll pardon me a moment, senorita—"

He tore open the envelope and read—

August 25, 1867

My dearest brother,

So long a time since I wrote, and no answer. I do hope nothing has happened to you in that terrible land. I tell myself I should not worry—that by now probably your plans have succeeded—maybe even now you are on your way back here with the money to pay our debts. Yet I can't help fearing—

Fortunately, the need is not so urgent now.

You see, Mr. Marshall—Brent—has been visiting Shelbourne Farm almost every weekend for two months now—and this past weekend did your little sister the great honor of asking for my hand in marriage.

Of course, I told him we would have to get the consent of the head of our family—which is yourself, dear Slade.

But I most fervently hope you approve—because I do love Brent Marshall with all my heart and want very much to become his wife.

So I do hope this reaches you—that you will let us know you approve—and I most fondly hope that you will be able to come home in time for the ceremony, which we would like to hold during the Christmas holidays.

(Incidentally, the matter of our indebtedness to the bank would become, of course, a family affair!)

Hoping—hoping—hoping to hear from you soon—and to have you here in December.

Your most affectionate and dutiful sister—

Nedra

Slade reread the parenthical paragraph.

So the recently concluded race—the entire expedition—had been unnecessary.

Or had it?

Of course not. Much as he liked Brent Marshall, Slade wasn't about to be beholden to him. He would take the ten-thousand back to Kentucky and clear Shelbourne Farm's debt. Then if Brent wanted to put some of the money back into the business, so they could buy more stock—

Perhaps California stock. Slade had been greatly impressed with Diablo Negro. The two incidents, the stallion losing his rider, Slade's encounter with Linc, just about canceled each other. Otherwise, the race was almost even.

But—glancing again at that paragraph—"a family affair" indeed! Typical feminine logic.

He chuckled.

"You have good news, senor?"

Juana Castillo was looking up at him with small vertical creases between her eyebrows.

"I guess so." He chuckled again. "My sister's going to get married—wants me to come back for the wedding."

"Oh—and you will go?"

There was an anxious note in her voice—her eyes searched his face.

"I guess I'll have to."

Her eyes dropped.

"And you senor—do you have a novia—a sweetheart—in—how you say?—Kentucky? Will you, too, be married?"

"Me? Good heavens no! As a matter of fact"—he looked around them—the room was filling with people—the musicians had struck up a lively tune—"as a matter of fact," he repeated, "I think I might come back to California."

"I hope you do, senor."

Her eyes smiled up at him—and for a fleeting instant he thought of other eyes—one with a tiny black mote—the eyes of the girl, Coco.

Then Juana Castillo's warm, soft hand took his.

"Will you dance with me, senor?"

Slade hung back.

"I'm afraid I don't know your style of dancing."

Turning toward the center of the room, where other couples were already whirling gaily over the highly polished red-tile flooring, the girl tossed a glowing smile over her shoulder.

"I will teach you, senor."

BLAZING WESTERN ADVENTURE BY *SPUR* AWARD WINNER NELSON NYE

2108-0	A LOST MINE NAMED SALVATION	$2.25
2150-1	BORN TO TROUBLE	$2.25
2214-1	QUICK-TRIGGER COUNTRY	$2.25
2253-2	CARTRIDGE CASE LAW	$2.25
2295-8	THE OVERLANDERS	$2.25

SUNDANCE
LEISURE'S ALL-TIME
BESTSELLING
WESTERN ADVENTURE SERIES

2105-6	SUNDANCE: HONCHO	$2.25
2138-2	SUNDANCE: BLOOD KNIFE	$2.25
2159-5	SUNDANCE: DEATH DANCE	$2.50
2181-1	SUNDANCE: GOLD STRIKE	$2.25
2203-6	SUNDANCE: LOS OLVIDADOS	$2.25
2223-0	SUNDANCE: SCORPION	$2.25
2285-0	SUNDANCE: APACHE WAR	$2.25

ZANE GREY'S FAMOUS CHARACTERS LIVE ON IN LEISURE'S ACTION-PACKED WESTERN SERIES BY HIS SON, ROMER ZANE GREY

2041-6 ZANE GREY'S LARAMIE NELSON:
THE OTHER SIDE OF THE CANYON $2.75

2082-3 ZANE GREY'S BUCK DUANE:
RIDER OF DISTANT TRAILS $2.75

2098-X ZANE GREY'S ARIZONA AMES:
GUN TROUBLE IN TONTO BASIN $2.75

2116-1 ZANE GREY'S LARAMIE NELSON:
THE LAWLESS LAND $2.75

2136-6 ZANE GREY'S BUCK DUANE:
KING OF THE RANGE $2.75

2158-7 ZANE GREY'S ARIZONA AMES:
KING OF THE OUTLAW HORDE $2.75

2192-7 ZANE GREY'S YAQUI:
SIEGE AT FORLORN RIVER $2.75

2213-3 ZANE GREY'S NEVADA JIM LACY:
BEYOND THE MOGOLLON RIM $2.75

MORE HARD-RIDING, STRAIGHT-SHOOTING WESTERN ADVENTURE FROM LEISURE BOOKS

2091-2	**THE OUTSIDE LAWMAN** Lee O. Miller	$2.25
2130-7	**VENGEANCE MOUNTAIN** R.C. House	$2.25
2149-8	**CANAVAN'S TRAIL** Burt and Budd Arthur	$2.25
2182-X	**BULLWHACKER** James D. Nichols	$2.25
2193-5	**VENGEANCE VALLEY** Allen Appel	$2.25
2204-4	**ENEMY IN SIGHT** Bill Bragg	$2.25
2233-8	**THE SUDDEN LAND** Dale Oldham	$2.25
2234-6	**CUTLER: MUSTANG** H.V. Elkin	$2.25
2243-5	**SHOWDOWN COUNTRY** Charlie Barstow	$2.25
2244-3	**PRAIRIE VENGEANCE** M.L. Warren	$2.25
2254-0	**RUSTLER'S BLOOD** David Everitt	$2.25
2263-X	**BROTHER GUN** Jack Slade	$2.25
2264-8	**CHASE A TALL SHADOW** John Ell	$2.25

Make the Most of Your Leisure Time
with
LEISURE BOOKS

Please send me the following titles:

Quantity	Book Number	Price
____	____	____
____	____	____
____	____	____
____	____	____

If out of stock on any of the above titles, please send me the alternate title(s) listed below:

Quantity	Book Number	Price
____	____	____
____	____	____
____	____	____
____	____	____

Postage & Handling ____

Total Enclosed $ ____

☐ Please send me a free catalog.

NAME_______________________________________

(please print)

ADDRESS ___________________________________

CITY _________________ STATE _________ ZIP _________

Please include $1.00 shipping and handling for the first book ordered and 25¢ for each book thereafter in the same order. All orders are shipped within approximately 4 weeks via postal service book rate. PAYMENT MUST ACCOMPANY ALL ORDERS.*

*Canadian orders must be paid in US dollars payable through a New York banking facility.

Mail coupon to: **Dorchester Publishing Co., Inc.**
6 East 39 Street, Suite 900
New York, NY 10016
Att: ORDER DEPT.